COWTOWN

By

Susan L. Pare

COWTOWN - All contents copyright © 2016 Susan L. Pare. All rights reserved. Printed in the United States of America.
First Edition October 2016
Second Edition April 2022
All rights reserved.

Cover designed by Susan L. Pare'
Paperback - ISBN-13:978-0-9966195-5-4

COWTOWN   Susan L. Paré

<u>MORE BOOKS BY THIS AUTHOR</u>

A Most Unusual Murder

The Finger

The Twisted Tree Triangle

The Box House

The Proof is in the Pudding

Blueberries and Bears and My Brother's Shoes

Red, White, and Blue (A Short Story)

She Never Stopped Talking

Red

The House on Ludington Street

What's Behind the Screen Door?

The Mayor's Son

Willerton Woods

Floating Face Down
A Sheriff "Cowboy" Berkson Mystery Novel – Book Three

Let's Play Autopsy

A Bad Week In Hollister
A Sheriff "Cowboy" Berkson Mystery Novel – Book Two

Don't Smother Your Mother
A Sheriff "Cowboy" Berkson Mystery Novel – Book One

Crossing Sydney

Index

Index... 3

Davies Park... 5

Chapter One 1

Chapter Two 5

Chapter Three 9

Chapter Four... 13

Chapter Five 17

Chapter Six.. 22

Chapter Seven... 28

Chapter Eight.. 32

Chapter Nine 36

Chapter Ten... 40

Chapter Eleven.. 44

Chapter Twelve 49

Chapter Thirteen 54

Chapter Fourteen 57

Chapter Fifteen 63

Chapter Sixteen 69

Chapter Seventeen 73

Chapter Eighteen... 78

Chapter Nineteen... 84

Chapter Twenty.. 90

Chapter Twenty-one 94

Chapter Twenty-two 100

Chapter Twenty-three 104

Chapter Twenty-four 113

Chapter Twenty-five 117

Chapter Twenty-six 124

Chapter Twenty-seven.................................... 131

Chapter Twenty-eight.................................... 133

Chapter Twenty-nine..................................... 140

Chapter Thirty... 145

Chapter Thirty-one 151

Chapter Thirty-two 159

Chapter Thirty-three 164

Chapter Thirty-four 169

Chapter Thirty-five 173

Chapter Thirty-six 177

Chapter Thirty-seven..................................... 181

Chapter Thirty-eight...................................... 185

Chapter Thirty-nine....................................... 190

Chapter Forty 197

Chapter Forty-one 202

Chapter Forty-Two... 207

Chapter Forty-three....................................... 211

About the Author 213

Davies Park

Columbus, Wisconsin is about thirty miles northeast of Madison, Wisconsin. In Columbus, on North Ludington Street near the Amtrak Station, there is a little park. It is called Davies Park.

The park is smaller now than it was when I played there. A sidewalk leads to a pretty little gazebo that was added years ago. The locals occasionally stop there to rest, spend time reading a favorite book, or just to contemplate their navels. A nice touch, which was added to the park, is a small book depository so people can share their books.

The land was donated to the town of Columbus by the Josiah Davies family many years ago after their house was moved to a lot by Highway 16, west of the town.

As you enter the park, to the left of the sidewalk, is a large rock with a plaque. The words 'Davies Park' are engraved on the plaque. This rock is shown on the back cover of the book.

My family moved to Columbus when I was in the fifth grade and we lived a couple of houses away from Davies Park. This was the playground for my siblings and me until we grew older and put away childish games.

The rock has been moved to a location near the main sidewalk, Way back then, it was situated further into the park and it was home plate. We stood in front of it when we swung that baseball bat and the trees were our bases. I spent a good part of my childhood there.

Some of the action in this novel takes place in a park and I had to give it a name. The park in this book is much larger and there's a lot more going on than the park in Columbus. (Thank the good lord.) But, I couldn't think of a better name for it than Davies Park.

So, when you read this book, know that such a place does exist. Sadly, many of the children, including a couple of my siblings, who played there so many years ago, do not.

Note: Except for the name of the park and the picture of the rock with a plaque on the cover, this has absolutely nothing to do with this book. I just thought you might find it interesting.

<u>Dedication</u>

To Patrick Michael McNulty – my dear friend.
This one's for you.

Time and distance are of no matter.

COWTOWN   Susan L. Paré

COWTOWN

COWTOWN   Susan L. Paré

<u>Chapter One</u>

Freddie 'Firecracker' Demonti stared at his brand-new Conquest Knight XV, which was parked in front of the Squirrel House Tavern. The right front and left back wheels were missing.

"What the fuck!" he exclaimed to himself. "How the hell did this happen?"

He looked around to see if anyone was watching him, turned, and walked back into the bar. "Pistol," he yelled at the bartender, "get Frank out here – now!"

"He just left," Pistol told Freddie. "He said he'd be back sometime this afternoon. You want I should call him?"

"I wanna see the security tapes. The one that's over the front door."

"What for?"

"What for? I'll tell you what for!" Freddie screamed. "Some asshole just stole two wheels off my truck. That's what for."

"No way. You're shitting me, right?" Pistol asked, trying not to laugh.

"Go take a look," Freddie yelled. "I wanna see the security video. Right now!"

"Okay. Okay. Settle down. The security system is in the back. Come with me."

"Who do you know that would have the guts to steal two wheels in broad daylight? Everyone around here knows that's my ride."

Pistol ignored Freddie's ranting and walked into the back room, which was a combination office and storage room. A huge desk was in the middle of the room, with ten filing cabinets of various sizes and colors crammed in behind it. Behind the door was a small table that held the security equipment. Pistol picked up the remote and hit a few buttons.

"Watch the monitor," Pistol told Freddie. A second later, the two men were looking at the front of the tavern on the monitor's screen.

"There we go," Pistol said. "You said you got here around 10:30 – right?"

"Around that," replied Freddie.

Pistol hit some more buttons on the remote and a video started playing, showing the activity happening in front of the tavern at 10:30 a.m. "Should be right about here," he commented. "See? There you are entering the bar."

"Of course, I see. What? You think I'm blind or something? How long will this take?" Freddie asked, impatiently.

"Not long. Keep watching. There's your car. It looks fine right there. Nobody's near it."

They watched as people passed in front of the camera but did not see anyone messing with Freddie's truck. A couple of people stopped for a few seconds to check it out, then continued on their way.

At 11:15, the monitor went dark. "What the hell just happened?" Freddie yelled at Pistol.

"Hold on. It might be a flaw on the disk. Keep watching."

At 11:21, the picture was back up on the monitor, showing the outside of the building with Freddie's vehicle in full view.

"Stop," Freddie yelled. "Son of a bitch! The wheels are gone. Back it up. Let's see that again."

"See what? There are six minutes when the

camera is blacked out. There's nothing to see. I guess while your tires were being removed, someone was holding something over the lens of the camera."

"I want to see where it went black again."

"Six minutes is a long time to jack two wheels. A couple of professionals could do it in a minute or so," commented Pistol.

"Play it again," Freddie demanded.

"I've got to get back to the bar," Pistol said. He walked over to the table that held the security equipment and pushed a few buttons. "If you want, I can make a copy of it for you."

"You're right. There's nothing to see. What good would a fucking copy do me?" Freddie whined.

"Maybe someone who knows what they're doing could make out what's going on. You know – like x-ray it or something."

"You seriously think they can see through whatever the hell was over the lens?"

"It's worth a try. I've got to go," Pistol said, as he left the room, grinning. What a dumb ass, he thought to himself.

Freddie Demonti hadn't been nicknamed 'Firecracker' because he liked fireworks. People called him that because he would explode over the slightest thing. He had a fast temper and the people in the neighborhood had learned to stay clear of him when Freddie was just a kid. More than one young boy had gone home with a black eye or a broken bone after messing with Freddie.

As a grown man, Freddie was a wannabe gangster whom people feared but had no respect for. He loved playing the horses and he was lucky. He bet big and he won big. He lived in a huge house, drove a bulletproof vehicle, and wore lots of gold chains. However, he still hadn't learned how to control his ferocious temper. Only now he used a baseball bat when he was fighting mad, instead of his fists.

He had never hit a woman. Even if he thought some broad had it coming, the thought of his mother finding out kept him under control. His mother was the one person he loved with all his heart and the only person that scared the bejusus out of him. He found out years ago that you didn't mess with mom.

He had never had a steady girlfriend, even though he had a great body and was extremely good-looking. There were plenty of women that he paid to satisfy his needs but he rarely screwed the same woman twice. One night with Freddie usually meant two days of recovery time for these prostitutes. Not because he was rough with them but because Freddie had a huge penis, which left them swollen and sore for days.

Freddie also liked getting his own way and, when he didn't, all hell would let loose.

Right now Freddie, still in Frank's office, was throwing everything he could get his hands on.

When Pistol heard the racket coming from the back room, he told the customers, who were drinking their lunch, to leave. When he mentioned that Freddie was having a hissy fit, they wasted no time heading for the door. Then, he picked up the phone and called Frank, his boss.

<u>Chapter Two</u>

"Are you okay?" Karlee asked.

"Hell, no, I'm not okay. If Firecracker finds out we were the ones who stole his tires, he'll totally kill us," Emmy Lou replied.

"He's not gonna find out."

"How can you be so sure? I just know someone will tell him it was us," Emmy Lou whined.

"No one will tell him. Everybody hates him," Karlee said, trying to reassure her.

"What if he offers a reward? Someone will tell so they can get the reward."

"Just relax, will you? We're fine."

Karlee Campanale wished she believed what she had just told her best friend, Emmy Lou. She knew if Firecracker ever found out who stole his tires, they were dead meat.

She glanced over at Rebecca and smiled. Karlee envied how cool her younger sister was, sound asleep on the couch. Emmy Lou and she were nervous wrecks and her sister was taking a nap.

"What should we do with them?" Emmy Lou asked.

"How the hell should I know."

"We could sell them."

"Oh, that's a fantastic idea, Emmy. Let's put signs up all over town saying we've got two tires for sale that fit a monster tank. I'm sure Firecracker will never put two and two together and figure out it was us that stole them."

"Well, we can't keep them here."

"I'll see if Mike can get rid of them for us. I figure

5

he owes us a favor," said Karlee.

"How do you figure that?"

Karlee smiled. "Because we just got even with Firecracker for beating him up," she answered.

"I think there's a big difference between getting beat up and stealing a couple of dumb tires," commented Emmy Lou.

"We got Firecracker where it hurts the most. You know how much he loves that big ass tank he drives. It's his baby. Well, guess what? His baby just got spanked."

"Can you imagine how mad he must be right now?" Emmy Lou said, laughing. "I bet his blood pressure is so high his head wants to explode."

"What's so funny?" Rebecca asked as she opened her big blue eyes.

"Sorry if we woke you," Karlee answered. "We're just trying to figure out how to get rid of the tires. Do you think Mike will get rid of them for us?"

"I figure he will," Rebecca answered, yawning. "Give him a call and see if he's up to it."

"He's gonna shit a brick when he finds out what we did," said Emmy Lou.

"Ya, he probably will," Karlee agreed.

"We could bury them in your backyard," Rebecca suggested. "Do you have any shovels?"

"No way. You're not digging up my yard," exclaimed Karlee.

"Too bad you don't have a garage. We could hide them there," Emmy Lou said.

"Well, I don't," replied Karlee. "I guess I better call Mike and see what he thinks. I want those damn tires out of my kitchen."

Rebecca grinned. "We sure as hell didn't think this through, did we?"

"Hey, it was a good idea at the time. It's the little things that always mess you up," stated Karlee.

"Well, I'm glad we stole them. He really hurt Mike and I think it was time someone stood up to that asshole."

"We didn't actually stand up to him, Rebecca."

"Whatever. Call Mike, will you?" Rebecca said.

"I'm on it," answered Karlee, as she reached for her phone. She waited for her brother to answer the call, then, frowned. "He must be on his phone. It went straight to voice mail."

"Tell him to call us as soon as possible," Emmy Lou said, as she glanced at her watch. "Shit, it's after three o'clock. I've got to get to work. Call me after you hear from him, will you?"

"You're bugging out on us?" Karlee asked.

"Sorry, gotta pay the bills. I'll talk to you later," Emmy Lou replied, gave them a wave, and walked out the front door.

Suddenly, Karlee yelled, "I've got it!"

Rebecca jumped. "God, Karlee. You scared me. What the hell are you yelling for?"

"I've got it."

"You've got what?" Rebecca asked.

"An idea. I've got an idea on how to get rid of the tires and embarrass the hell out of Firecracker."

"You don't think he's already embarrassed that someone took his tires?"

"Not embarrassed enough."

"You're gonna get us killed with your stupid ideas. Isn't it bad enough that we've got his tires in your kitchen? Now, you want to push his buttons even further?"

"Listen. How about this?"

"What?" Rebecca replied, sighing.

"We use them for planters."

"We do what? What the hell are you talking about?" Rebecca asked.

"We'll need some dirt. A couple of bags should do it. And, two huge dildos. I mean the biggest dildos we can find. And, plants. We need a couple of plants with flowers to add some color.

Rebecca thought about what her sister had said and, then, grinned. "You are so bad," she told Karlee.

"We'll need Mike to get the dildos. I'm sure as hell not going into a porn shop. He should probably drive over to Brownsville. No one knows him there. I'll get the dirt. I can pick that up at Home Depot."

"I'll go with you. We'll get some plants while we're there."

Karlie thought for a minute. "We'll need a lookout. No, not a lookout. A spy. We'll need someone who can spy on Firecracker. He'll probably be at the Squirrel House tonight, just like every night. Emmy Lou could go and have a drink and keep an eye on him. If he leaves before we're done, she can call and warn us."

"Do you think she'll do it?"

"Of course, she will," Karlee answered.

"What time does she get off work?"

"I think this is her day for a short shift, so probably around ten or so. I'll give her a call and find out for sure after I talk to Mike."

"Do you have a place in mind?" Rebecca asked.

"Oh, indeed I do, sister. Indeed, I do."

Chapter Three

Mike Campanale ended his call and checked to see who had called him while he had been talking to his business partner. He listened to Karlee's voice mail message and smiled. She mentioned that it was urgent and he should call her back as soon as possible. Everything with Karlee was urgent, Mike thought.

He lit a cigarette and immediately put it out. I'm never going to be able to quit smoking if I don't quit buying these damn things, he thought. The first one today, though. It's Karlee's fault. She always gets me nervous.

He hit a speed number on his cell and waited for Karlee to answer.

"Mike, what the hell are you doing? I've been waiting forever for you to call."

"I've got a job, you know. Besides, you only called ten minutes ago. What's so important?"

"I need you to drive over to Brownsville for me. There's a porno shop there that sells all kinds of sex stuff. I need two of the biggest dildos you can find."

Mike chuckled to himself, wondering what the hell his sister was up to now. He was grinning, as he asked the obvious question. "One isn't enough for you?"

Karlee laughed. "It isn't for me."

"What the hell are you up to, Karlee?"

"Are you sitting down? I don't think what I'm gonna tell you is going to make you very happy. But we need your help."

"Why do you need my help? Or, better yet, what have you done now?"

"Okay, this is what happened. You know

Firecracker, right? Forget I said that. Of course, you know him. He just beat the hell out of you a couple of weeks ago."

"Karlee, what did you do?" Mike asked, emphasizing each word.

"Well, you know – I mean – well, you know that big ass ride that Firecracker owns?"

"Of course. Everybody in town knows he owns that tank. What about it?"

"Well – now, don't get mad but it seems that a couple of his tires were ripped off today. Right in front of the Squirrel House Tavern. And, in broad daylight, too, while Firecracker was inside drinking his breakfast."

Mike took a deep breath. Please, dear Lord, he thought, don't let her tell me she did it. "Really," he said, calmly. "And, why should this be of any interest to me?"

"Well – you know Emmy Lou Larson, right?"

"Yes. I know her. In fact, Karlee, we went out a few times, if you recall."

"Oh, that's right. Anyway, Emmy Lou, Rebecca, and I thought it would be cool if we got even for what he did to you."

"So, you're fighting my fights now?"

"Well, kind of. Plus, we wanted to see how fast we could take the tires off his truck."

"Please, don't tell me you three numb nuts stole his tires."

"Just two of them. Rebecca and I took them off, while Emmy Lou blocked out the surveillance camera's lens. Smart, huh? No one can tell it was us."

Mike sighed a deep sigh. "No, Karlee. Not smart. Dumb. That was really dumb."

"Wait," Karlee interrupted. "I'm not done. We did it in under six minutes, Mike. We had those two tires off in less than six minutes. Pretty damn good, right?"

"You do know I'm talking to a dead person, don't you?"

"We're fine. Nobody is gonna tell Firecracker it was us. Anyway, we need a couple of huge – like, humungous – dildos. Will you get them for us?

"Why would I do that, Karlee?"

"Well – you see the tires are in my kitchen and I've got to get rid of them. There's no good place to hide them, so we figured we'd put them to good use."

"I don't want to know," Mike yelled, into his phone. "Don't tell me another thing."

"So, you don't want to know what we need the dildos for?"

"No, I don't."

"Will you get them? We need them no later than ten tonight. I'll pay you back."

"No, Karlee, I won't," Mike answered.

"Why not? You have to get them, Mike. Please. Come on, help us out. We stole those tires to get even with Firecracker for hurting you. We did it for you. Please, Mike."

Mike sat back in his chair and stared at his phone. He had two sisters who had spent the better part of their lives trying to drive him crazy. Right now, he figured they were succeeding. He pictured the three women in front of the bar, stealing tires off Firecracker's tank in broad daylight. They had balls, he thought. What the hell? Why not? "How big, did you say?" he asked Karlee.

Karlee squealed with joy. "I knew you'd help us.

Thank you, bro'. When will you be here?"

"In a few hours. I gather you suggested I drive to Brownsville, where no one knows me, to do my shopping?"

"You know it," replied Karlee. "Oh, wait, Mike. There's one more thing."

Mike shook his head in despair. "What?"

"Do you know how to remove tires from their rims?"

Chapter Four

Freddie watched his SUV being hauled away. He had spent the last few hours on the phone trying to locate a towing company that had a flatbed truck available. He finally found one who was willing to drive across town but only after he said he'd pay extra. A tow truck was out of the question, due to the vehicle being lopsided with two tires missing.

He sat down on the stoop in front of the Squirrel House Tavern and reflected on his day.

First, he thought, somebody has the fucking nerve to steal two wheels off my ride. Second, Frank kicks me out of his tavern just because I got a little upset and broke a few things in his office. Third, I've just spent hours, standing here on the sidewalk in the hot sun, trying to find a tow truck to take my vehicle to the dealer. And to top it off, Hermus Car Rental only has a Prius left on their lot. A fucking Prius, for god's sake. I can't be seen driving around in a little shit car like that. It's bad enough that the word is out about me being ripped off.

Freddie sighed. He watched the traffic go by, wondering what his next move should be. He pulled his phone out of his pocket, hit speed dial number one, and waited.

"Ma," he said, whining. "I'm having a really bad day. Can you come and get me?"

"What's wrong, baby?"

"Someone stole a couple of tires off my truck and I need a ride."

"Are you kidding me? Who would do that?"

"If I fucking knew, I'd bust their fucking heads in."

"Watch your mouth, Frederick. You're not too old to be slapped, you know."

"Sorry, Ma. It's just that I'm so blanking mad I can hardly see straight."

"That's okay, baby. Now, here's what we're gonna do. You call the dealer where you bought your car and tell them you need a loaner while they are fixing yours. I'll come get you and drive you over there so you can pick up the loaner. How does that sound?"

Freddie shook his head in frustration, wondering why he hadn't thought of that. Of course, the dealer had loaner cars that customers used while their vehicles were being repaired. "Sounds great, Ma. I don't know why I didn't think of that."

"Well, baby, you can't be expected to think of everything. That's what mothers are for."

"Right," Freddie muttered. "So, how long before you get here?"

"Well, I don't rightly know, seeing as how I don't know where you are," his mother answered.

"I'm in front of the Squirrel House. I'll watch for you."

"It will probably be a half hour or so. I need to comb my hair and put on some lipstick. I should probably let Millie out for a pee before I leave."

Freddie rolled his eyes and sighed. "Okay, Ma. See you in a bit."

"You should go inside and sit for a while. You shouldn't be out in this heat for too long," his mother suggested.

"I'm fine. Just get going, will ya?" Freddie said, raising his voice.

"Don't yell at me, young man."

"Sorry, Ma."

"Well, I should hope so. I thought I raised you better than that."

"You did, Ma. You did a wonderful job. It's just that . . ."

"Ya, I know,' his mother interrupted. "It's just that you're so fucking mad."

Freddie's mouth dropped open in shock. He couldn't believe his mother had just dropped the f-bomb. "Ma, did you just say fuck?" he asked. "Ma? Are you still there?"

Freddie wasn't one to stay at home watching TV, especially on a Saturday night. So, a little before ten, Freddie parked his loaner car in front of the Squirrel House Tavern, wondering if it was safe to go in and get a drink. He decided to chance it, hoping that Frank wasn't working tonight. Or, if he was, that he was over his mad. Freddie had an envelope with twenty one-hundred-dollar bills inside to give to Frank. He hoped that would cover the cost of the damage that he had done earlier in the day.

As he walked into the bar, the first person he saw was Pistol. He must be doing a double, Freddie thought. I wonder if Frank is shorthanded. He waved to a couple of guys he knew, who were sitting at a table, and plunked his ass down on an empty barstool.

"You've got some nerve," Pistol said, as he walked toward Freddie.

"Is Frank around?" Freddie asked.

"He might be. Why?"

"I've got something for him," Freddie answered and handed him the envelope.

"It better be something good."

"It is. How about a scotch on the rocks?"

"In a minute. Let me see what Frank has to say about you being here," Pistol remarked and walked away.

Freddie swung the stool around to face the customers sitting at tables and took it all in. He noticed a woman sitting alone in a booth, talking on her phone. She looked familiar but he couldn't put a name with the face. He watched her for a few minutes. As he turned back to the bar, he noticed Pistol walking toward him.

"Scotch – right?" Pistol asked.

"Right," replied Freddie with a big grin. "On the rocks, please."

Emmy Lou looked up from her phone and glanced over at the bar. Pistol was handing Freddie a drink. "He's here. He just got his first drink. It's time for you to move out."

Chapter Five

In the western section of the City of Chicago, there is an area known as Cowtown. The residents who live there don't acknowledge that they live in Chicago and consider Cowtown a totally separate entity. At least they do until their annual property tax bills arrive. Then, it is a hard reminder that they are residents of Chicago paying steep Chicago taxes. Although they hate to admit it, Cowtown is no different than other Chicago neighborhoods, such as Wrigleyville or Hyde Park.

Frontier Street – sometimes called Main Street – is the heart of Cowtown. Frontier Street is lined with big maple trees and in the fall, when the leaves on the maple trees turn color, the view is spectacular. The street has a few quaint shops, some restaurants and taverns, a mom-and-pop grocery store, and several churches.

Davies Park, named after John Davies, the man who donated the land, is located on Frontier Street. It is the size of a city block and the residents keep it as clean as a freshly bathed baby's butt. It's where most of the town's summer activities are held. There is a bandstand in the middle of the park and usually on a Friday night some little-known band, hoping for their big break, entertain the locals.

Farmers' Market is held in Davies Park every Friday, Saturday, and Sunday from late May to early October, weather permitting. The churches on Frontier Street continuously try to block the market from operating during Sunday church hours, saying it is disruptive to their services and sacrilegious. Every year the churches near the park petition the City of Chicago to ban Sunday morning market sales and every year they are ignored. A few ministers have been known to actually pray for a thunderstorm during their service, hoping the rain will wash away all the sinners who shop at the market on Sunday mornings.

The morning after his tires were stolen, Freddie picked up his mom to take her to church. He was tempted to drop her off at the front door, go back home, and jump back into bed. He had stayed at the Squirrel House until last call and his head was killing him. He smiled when he thought about the woman he had met. Although he didn't get lucky, he did get her phone number. Emmy something was her name. He definitely would be giving her a call. He glanced over at his mother and wondered how pissed off she'd be if he didn't go to church with her.

"What's that sigh for?"

Freddie shrugged. "Nothing. Just thinking, that's all."

"Well, stop it and concentrate on your driving."

"Do you see a parking spot?" Freddie asked.

His mother glanced around and, then, exclaimed, "There's one! It's right in front of the park entrance. Park there!"

"It's on the other side of the street."

"So what? Turn the car around."

Freddie slowly passed the parking spot, then pulled a uey in the middle of the street and parked the car. "Happy now?" he asked his mother.

"Best parking spot in town," she said smugly. "Henrietta Hapers will be so jealous."

"You know, Mom, I really don't feel too good.

Maybe, I'll skip church this morning. I'll pick you up later or maybe you can get a ride home."

Freddie's mother turned in her seat and glared at him. "If you were well enough to go out drinking half the night, you're well enough to go to church. Now, tuck your shirt in and get your ass out of the car. You're going to church."

Freddie held her gaze for a couple of seconds before he looked away and muttered, "I have a headache."

"You are a headache. Now, let's go." She waited a moment. "Now, Freddie."

Freddie sighed again and opened the car door. "Alright, I'm coming," he whined.

As Freddie and his mother walked toward St. John's Catholic Church, they noticed quite a few people talking and laughing near the bandstand.

"What do you suppose is going on?" Freddie's mother asked.

"How would I know? You want to walk over there and take a look?" he replied.

"Do we have enough time?" Mrs. Demonti inquired, not wanting to miss the beginning of the church service. On the other hand, she really wanted to see what was going on in the park.

"Come on, Ma. Let's go see what the big deal is."

Freddie and his mom walked over to the bandstand. A couple of the onlookers glanced at them and sniggered. A few said good morning and moved out of the way, making room for Freddie and his mother.

On each side of the bandstand steps, which led up to the stage, was a tire filled with dirt. Ten Impatiens plants, in full bloom, encircled the inside of each tire.

Placed directly in the middle was a huge multicolored dildo, its tip facing up to the sky.

Mrs. Demonti frowned, not understanding what was so funny. She turned to a woman standing next to her and quietly asked, "Why is everyone laughing? I think the arrangements are very pretty."

The woman fought to hold her composure, failed, and started laughing. "I'm so sor . . ." She took a deep breath and tried again to talk without laughing. "I'm sor. . ." Still laughing, she turned away from Mrs. Demonti and walked away.

Mrs. Demonti turned around to look at Freddie and immediately backed up. She had seen that look on his face enough times to know Freddie was about to blow. She reached out and grabbed his hand. "Come on, Freddie, let's go."

Freddie shook her hand loose and stepped up to a middle-aged man. "Did you do this?" he yelled.

"Hey, man – back off. I'm just looking," the man replied.

"Who did this?" Freddie yelled loudly. "Which one of you perverts did this?"

The crowd started walking away from the bandstand, not wanting to be the next person who was a target of Freddie's temper.

"Hey, mister."

Freddie turned to see who was talking to him and saw a young boy, about eleven years old, standing behind him.

"Get away from me, kid," Freddie said.

"Are those the tires that got stole off your truck?"

Freddie reached out and grabbed the boy by his shirt and pulled him in close. "What do you know about any tires?" he asked.

"Freddie, let him go," Mrs. Demonti yelled. "He's just a kid."

"Ya, mister, put me down!" the boy screamed, as Freddie lifted him off his feet by the front of his shirt.

"Put him down. Now!" a man's voice bellowed.

As Freddie turned around to see who was yelling at him, he was punched in the face by a fist. He dropped the boy, who went running to the man, obviously his father.

"Do you know who I am?" Freddie shouted, wiping away the blood that was dripping out of his nose. "You're dead meat, you fucking prick."

"Ya, I know who you are. You're that idiot people call Firecracker. You think you're some big deal around here, don't you? Well, you know what I think?" the man asked. "I think they call you Firecracker because you go off before you even get your dick out."

Freddie stared at the man, his face turning beat red. "I'm gonna fucking kill you," he stammered.

"You wanna start up with me? Come on, tough guy. Go for it."

Freddie stepped back a couple of steps and sized the man up. He glanced over at his mother, feeling bad that she had to see what was about to happen. But that little feeling of empathy only lasted a second before Freddie went for it.

Chapter Six

Karlee and Rebecca had arrived at Davies Park before the Farmer's Market opened. They had stopped at a Dunkin' Donuts and picked up half a dozen donuts and a couple of containers of coffee. Seeing it was so early, they had their pick of which park bench to sit on. They chose one that wasn't next to their 'artwork', but close enough so they could hear people's comments when they saw the tires.

They had been sitting there for about thirty minutes before the first person noticed the tires. After that, there had been a steady parade of people gawking at the exhibit and making one hilarious statement after another.

Interestingly enough, no one had reached down to remove the dildos, even though some parents had their children with them.

"I'm gonna pee my pants," Rebecca said, laughing. "God, this is better than the circus."

"Shh," said Karlee. "I can't hear over your laughter."

"I can't believe that almost everyone knows that those are Firecracker's tires," Rebecca said. "Man, word travels fast in this town."

"No one has mentioned us, though. I wonder if anyone knows that it was us who stole the tires."

"Good point," said Rebecca. "Just look at those beautiful dildos. Mike outdid himself this time. Who knew that they made Gay Pride colored dildos."

Karlee laughed. "The best part is the tip being red. It could have been reversed with the blue on top and red on the bottom. I like a red tip, don't you?"

Rebecca snorted as she laughed. "I'll take any colored tip," she replied, cracking Karlee up.

Karlee took a deep breath, trying to regain her composure. "God, Becca, I haven't laughed this hard in ages." She started to take a drink of her coffee but stopped when she noticed Freddie and his mother walking towards the bandstand.

"Becca," she said, nudging her sister. "Look who's here."

Rebecca glanced over to where Karlee motioned. "Holy crap," she exclaimed. "This couldn't get any better. Now the show really begins."

A few minutes later, they saw Freddie get punched in the face by some man they didn't recognize. Rebecca grabbed her sister's arm and squeezed it.

"Did you see that? He got punched out," Rebecca exclaimed.

"He deserved it for grabbing that kid. Wait a minute. Look! They're fighting," Karlee exclaimed.

At the exact moment that Freddie went for it, his mother decided it was time to stop the argument between the two men. She made the huge mistake of stepping between them and was the recipient of Freddie's fist. The blow lifted her off her feet and onto her ass. She hit the cement sidewalk hard, which knocked the wind out of her.

The look of terror on Freddie's face was straight out of a horror movie. As he started to bend down to help his mother, the man he had been arguing with landed a solid blow to Freddie's chin.

Freddie Demonti had not earned his reputation for being a bully for no reason. He knew how to fight, and he knew how to fight dirty. Anyone in the neighborhood, who had been beaten up by Freddie and could still walk, considered himself lucky. When the man hit Freddie for the second time, in Freddie's mind that person was already dead.

Freddie lost total control over reason and hit the guy hard, knocking him down. Then, he proceeded to kick the living shit out of him.

The young boy was screaming at Freddie to stop hurting his dad and for someone to help him. It took four men to pull Freddie off the man, who was now curled up into a ball trying to protect himself.

Freddie's mother was lying on the ground, trying to catch her breath. A couple of women finally bent down and helped her to a bench.

Karlee glanced over at her sister, who looked like she was going to cry. "We should go, Becca."

"That man is hurt bad. Shouldn't we call 911 for help?"

"I think someone already did. Let's just get out of here."

"What did we do, Karlee? No one was supposed to get hurt."

"We couldn't have known this would happen, Becca. Don't blame yourself. We had no way of knowing Freddie would show up here this morning."

"Well, he did. And, now look at what happened because of our stupid joke."

Karlee took her sister's arm and turned so she was facing her. "Listen. This is not our fault. I'm sorry that someone got hurt but Freddie deserved this. Don't forget what he did to Mike."

"I know," Rebecca said. "I hope his mother is alright."

"Hey, she raised that piece of shit. It's probably her fault that he's like the way he is. I don't feel sorry for her one little bit. Come on. Let's get out of here."

Just as Rebecca and Karlee were about to leave, the paramedics arrived. Curiosity overruled their better judgment and they stayed to watch the paramedics attend to the injured man, who was still curled up on the ground.

A few minutes later, a second ambulance arrived, sirens blasting, and two more paramedics, pushing a gurney, ran into the park. They helped lift the injured man onto the gurney and wheeled him to the waiting ambulance.

Freddie's mom, who was still having trouble breathing, was finally attended to by a paramedic. Freddie mentioned to him that his mother had been punched in the face and had landed hard on her ass. After checking her jaw, the paramedic told Freddie that it would be a good idea if she was also transported to the hospital for x-rays, just to be sure her jaw wasn't broken.

Freddie watched as his mother was being helped to an ambulance. "I'll come with you, Mom," he said.

"Sorry, sir," said the paramedic. "You can't ride with us. You'll need to stay here to talk to the police."

"I need to be with my mom," Freddie stated. "She needs me."

"This is the man you need to talk to," the paramedic shouted, pointing at Freddie.

Freddie turned to see who the paramedic was yelling at and saw two Chicago cops approaching him. Knowing he could be in big trouble and possibly facing a battery charge, Freddie took a deep breath and tried to get his temper under control.

He looked around and realized that almost everyone who had been there, when the fight started, had left the area. Then, he noticed two women sitting on a bench staring at him. He stared back and smiled at them.

"He really is good-looking, isn't he," Rebecca said. "Just look at that smile."

"Yes. And, he has a body like a Greek god," Karlee responded. "What? You got the hots for him now?"

Rebecca laughed. "It would be interesting, wouldn't it? I wonder if he's as big as people say."

Karlee looked her sister in the eye. "Don't get any ideas, Becca. I mean it."

Rebecca grinned. "I'm joking. You don't have to worry about me."

"I always have to worry about you."

Rebecca glanced over at Freddie. "He's still staring at us," she said.

"Let's go."

"Wait a minute. The cops are here," Rebecca commented. "Maybe we should stay and talk to them."

"Come on. Let's get the hell out of here. I'm not giving the cops a statement."

As the two women stood up to leave, Freddie walked toward them. "Hi," he greeted them. "You're not leaving, are you?"

"Sorry, we've got to go," said Karlee.

"Do you think you could stay a little longer and talk to the cops? You know, tell them that I didn't start it and that the guy hit me first."

"Sorry," Karlee said again. "We didn't see anything. We can't help you out."

"You must have seen that guy hit me," Freddie said.

"You mean after you picked his kid up by the front of his shirt? Nope, we didn't see that or anything else," Karlee replied, sarcastically.

"Come on, Karlee, let's get out of here," Rebecca said.

"Please," Freddie pleaded. "I could really use . . ." He stopped talking as the women turned their backs to him and walked away.

Chapter Seven

People in Cowtown breathed a little easier for the next six months, knowing that Freddie Demonti was spending time in jail. He had been found guilty of assault on Steve Martinson, the man Freddie had beat up.

The judge told Freddie that he should consider himself lucky that the prosecuting attorney had allowed him to plead down from a battery charge to the lesser charge of assault. The fact that Mr. Martinson had landed the first blow played in Freddie's favor. However, Freddie was the only one charged with a crime and was sentenced to six months in county jail.

Freddie's first few weeks in jail were rough. His fast temper got him into more than a few fights. He finally realized that he better learn to control his mouth and get along with his fellow inmates if he wanted to survive. The fact that Freddie had money – lots of money – helped. By the time Freddie was released from jail, half of the guards had become his best friends.

During Freddie's incarceration, he had three cellmates. The first two were quiet men and they were in and out of his life within a few weeks. The third one, Monty Miller, never shut up. By the time Freddie was released, he knew everything about Monty. starting with the day he was born. Thanks to Monty, Freddie also knew which guard was single, married, divorced, and how many kids he had. He knew what every fellow inmate was in jail for and the length of their sentences. Freddie also knew that it had been three women who had stolen the two tires off his truck but he only had two of their names.

Freddie wasn't the type of person who forgave and forgot. Once you crossed him, you were on his shit list forever. So, his problem wasn't wondering if he should punish these three broads when he got out of jail but how. In his entire life, Freddie had never intentionally hurt a woman but things were about to change.

The first thing Freddie did, after being released from jail, was to spend an hour soaking in his oversized bathtub. He called his mother, while surrounded by bubbles, and asked if she'd like to go out for dinner. She suggested she cook instead and Freddie grabbed at the chance for a home-cooked meal.

Once out of the tub, Freddie started searching for a napkin that had a phone number written on it. He went through the pockets of every pair of pants hanging in his closet without finding it. Freddie sat down on his bed trying to think. He lay back on his bed and smiled as the name on the napkin finally came to him. Emmy Lou. She had to be the third woman. Now he had all the names.

At 10:30, Freddie parked his truck in front of the Squirrel House Tavern and shut off the engine. He belched and the taste of his mother's pot roast filled his mouth. He glanced in the rearview mirror and decided he looked great. I mean, like how could I possibly improve upon perfection, he thought, laughing to himself. He looked a little pale but he figured a couple of tanning sessions would take care of that.

At 10:32, Freddie exited his vehicle and started to walk up the few steps that led into the bar. A shot rang out and Freddie lurched forward, hands out, trusting that the door would stop his fall. However, a man who was leaving the bar opened the door at that precise moment and Freddie fell forward.

"What the fuck?" Freddie yelled as he landed flat on his face.

The man, surprised by Freddie's abrupt entrance, stepped back into his wife who was behind him. She shrieked, as she landed hard on the bar floor.

Pistol, who was tending bar that night, glanced over at the door to see what the noise was all about. Thinking that a fight had started, he reached for the baseball bat that was kept under the bar and headed for the door.

"Whoa!" the man yelled, holding his hands in the air, as Pistol came towards them with the bat raised in a threatening manner. "I believe this man's been shot."

Pistol stopped, looked at Freddie who was lying face down on the floor, and bent over to talk to him. "Mister, can you hear me?" he asked.

Freddie turned his head towards Pistol's shoes and tried to look up. "Pistol?"

"Oh, my god! Freddie, is that you?" Pistol asked, shocked at seeing who was lying there.

"Sure is. How ya doing, Pistol?"

"Better than you. You're bleeding."

"I guess. You wanna call 911? I think some son of a bitch just shot me." Freddie said.

"Who was it?" Pistol asked.

"Damned if I know. Do you mind making that call now?" Freddie asked.

"Ya, right away. Sorry." Pistol looked over at a man who was sitting at the bar, watching the disturbance. "Hey, Gary, call 911 and tell them we need an ambulance," he yelled.

"Got it," Gary replied, took out his cell phone, and made the call.

"Bring me some towels, too," Pistol yelled.

Gary finished the call, went behind the bar, got a handful of towels, walked over, and handed them to Pistol. "Is that Firecracker?" he asked Pistol.

"Sure is," Pistol told him.

"When did he get out? I thought he was in jail."

"I don't know. Hey, Freddie, when did you get out?"

Freddie, head still on the floor, glanced up at Pistol and smiled. Then, he shuddered and lost consciousness.

Pistol gently lifted Freddie's head a few inches off the floor and placed the towels under him.

Pistol looked up toward the ceiling and let out a deep sigh. He closed his eyes and silently prayed that the trip to the hospital would be Freddie's final ride.

Chapter Eight

"Freddie Demonti is out of jail."

"Already? When did he get out?" Karlee asked.

"Yesterday," her brother answered.

"That time flew by."

"He's in the hospital. He got shot last night as he was going into the Squirrel House."

"Is he dead?" Karlee inquired.

"No," Mike said. "I just said that he was in the hospital."

"Too bad."

"Seriously, Karlee? You hate him that much?"

"He hurt you, Mike. Damn right I hate that prick. Who shot him?"

"I don't know. It could be anybody. There aren't many people around here that like him."

"I'd shoot him," Karlee commented.

"You would not. And, you better not let anyone hear you talking like that."

"Why not? I'm not the one who shot him."

"I'm gonna go visit him."

"At the hospital?"

"Yep."

"You are not," Karlee said. "You hate him. Why would you visit him?"

"I'm his insurance guy. Or, at least, I was. I want to let him know that his health insurance expired while he was in jail."

"Are you kidding me?" Karlee said laughing. "Anyway, I doubt they'll let you in his room."

"It's Sunday. What else do I have to do?"

"Mike, listen to me. Do not go visit him. You'll just

draw attention to yourself. It's a nice day. Why don't you go visit mom and dad?"

"I'm not in the mood. I don't feel like going over there just to hear her complain about – well, everything."

"Hey, if I had us for kids I'd be complaining, too."

"I'd like to find out how Firecracker is doing," Mike said, changing the subject back to their original conversation. "You want to take a ride and go with me?"

"No, I do not want to take a ride with you. You're an idiot if you go to the hospital. How about we go to The Plantation for dinner tonight? I'll give Becca a call and see if she wants to go with us."

"Sorry, I can't. I've got a date tonight."

"Who's the lucky lady?

"Emmy Lou," Mike told her.

"Really? So, you two are starting up again. Interesting."

"Bye, Karlee," Mike said.

"Wait. I want to hear more about you and Emmy Lou. Mike? Mike, are you still there?"

Freddie opened his eyes and quickly shut them when the bright light made him squint.

"Good. You're awake. How do you feel?" a soft feminine voice asked.

Freddie smiled at the question. How the hell did she think he felt after being shot? He gently opened his eyes and looked at the nurse who was standing at the foot of his bed.

"Not too bad. The light bothers my eyes, though."

"I'll pull the drapes. How's the pain on a scale of one to ten?" she asked.

"Maybe a five. It's tolerable," Freddie replied.

"Good. You're lucky, you know. The bullet was a through and through."

"What kind of bullet was it?" Freddie inquired.

"You'll have to ask the doctor about that, sweetie. I'm just here to take care of you. I don't have that information."

"When will the doc be in to see me?"

"Soon. He usually makes his rounds early. In the meantime, why don't you just close those pretty brown eyes of yours and take a nap?"

"Can I have something for the pain?" Freddy asked, giving her his best smile.

"I just gave you something. You'll probably be sleeping before I even leave the room."

She smiled at him, watched him close his eyes, and drift off. She walked over to the side of the bed, pulled back the covers, and stared. She grinned, as she took in the wondrous sight. They're right, she thought. That dick could definitely do some serious damage. She stuck out her index finger and poked it.

"Are you enjoying yourself, Cindi?"

Cindi jumped and turned toward the door.

"You scared the crap out of me, Doctor. Don't you ever knock?"

"Don't need to. I'm a doctor," he said smiling. "What the hell were you doing just now?"

Cindi grinned. "I had to see for myself if the rumor was true. I have to say, that's the biggest dick I've ever seen. And, believe me, I've seen a lot of them."

"I imagine you have. Both in and out of the hospital," the doctor remarked.

Cindi laughed. "Let's not get personal."

"How's the patient doing, anyway?"

"I just gave him some pain medication. He'll be out for a while. When I talked to him, he seemed to be alert and not in too much pain."

"Are his vitals okay?"

"His vitals are fine, doctor," Cindi answered. "Almost everything is normal."

"Almost?"

"Well, you certainly can't call what is hanging between his legs normal, can you?"

The doctor laughed. "Not in a million years."

Chapter Nine

Freddie spent the next two days in the hospital recovering from his gunshot wound. He had charmed every nurse that had attended to his needs and dozens more who just 'happened to stop by' to see how he was doing. By the time he was released, he had the phone numbers of at least a dozen nurses who wanted him to call them.

Freddie was glad to be home. His mother greeted him when he arrived, gave him a big hug, and told him that everything would be okay, now that she was there to take care of him.

"Take it easy, Ma," Freddie told his mother. "You can't hug me that hard. My shoulder still hurts, you know."

"Sorry, Baby. It's just that I'm so relieved you're still with me. That bullet could have killed you. I love you so much," she said, tears filling her eyes.

"I know, Ma. I love you, too. Now, how about you get me a nice cold beer?"

"Is it okay for you to have alcohol?" she asked.

"It's fine. A beer isn't going to kill me."

"Well, I don't know if you should be drinking. That doesn't seem like a good idea to me."

"Never mind, Ma," Freddie said, aggravated at his mother for arguing with him. "I'll get it myself,"

"You don't have to get huffy," his mother said. "I'll get it."

Freddie watched his mother as she walked out of the room to the kitchen. I love that woman, he thought, but there are days when she drives me nuts.

"Hey, Mom," Freddie yelled. "How about making

me something to eat?"

A week after Freddie was shot, he was back at work at his pawnshop in Chicago. Although he spent the better part of his days running the store, the majority of his income came from loan sharking. Freddie loaned money to desperate people, at exorbitant interest rates, and showed no mercy when they failed to pay him on time. When he first started in the business, he had no qualms about breaking a few arms or legs. Now, he had a couple of enforcers who did the dirty work for him.

However, when it was personal, like messing with his ride and stealing his tires, Freddie fought his own fights. Freddie's problem right now wasn't if he should get even with those three bitches that stole his tires and made planters out of them – it was how. He just didn't know if he could beat the crap out of a woman.

Maybe I should just screw the hell out of them, Freddie thought, smiling to himself. Not being able to walk for a week might just teach them not to mess around with Freddie Demonti.

Freddie started to hit the brakes, changed his mind, and accelerated through the stoplight. He made a mental note that he better start paying attention to his driving and stop thinking about those women.

Freddie slowed down, looked for oncoming traffic, saw none, and made a left turn onto Frontier Street. Suddenly, he hit the brakes, coming to a hard stop. He couldn't believe his eyes. There, standing at the intersection was the woman he had met at the Squirrel House. He drove the short distance to where she was standing, pulled up beside her, and put down the passenger side window.

"Emmy Lou. Right?" he said smiling.

Emmy Lou looked over at the truck and took a couple of steps backward. She stared at the vehicle and immediately felt sick to her stomach.

"Remember me?" Freddie asked. "We met about seven months ago at the Squirrel House. I'm Freddie Demonti."

Emmy Lou gave him a weak smile. "Sure, I remember you. How are you doing?"

"I'm doing good, Emmy Lou. I really am. I'm glad I ran into you. I would have called you but I lost your phone number."

"That's okay," Emmy replied and jumped as a car behind Freddie blew its horn.

"You need a lift?" Freddie asked her.

"I'm good. Thanks, anyway," Emmy Lou replied.

"Get in. I'll give you a ride to wherever you want to go."

"Thanks, uh - Freddie. I'm, uh – I really can't. I mean. . ." Emmy Lou gave Freddie a little smile. "Sorry. I mean, I'm just going to the next block. I don't need a ride for that."

"Then, how about giving me your phone number? I promise I won't lose it this time."

"I'm sorry but I'm seeing someone. I've got to get going and it looks like you're holding up traffic. You should probably move your car."

"So, who are you seeing? Do I know the guy?"

"I doubt it," Emmy Lou said and then jumped as the horn scared her again.

Freddie opened his car door and got out. Emmy Lou watched as he walked to the car behind him. She couldn't hear their conversation, so when the car pulled around Freddie's truck, she was surprised. She had expected to see Freddie slug the guy. Freddie walked back to his truck and got in. He leaned over, so he could see out of the passenger window.

"Sorry about that. You sure I can't drop you somewhere?" he asked again, smiling.

"I'm sure."

"I'd like to see you again," Freddie said, turning on the charm.

"Sorry. As I said, I'm seeing someone. See you around," Emmy Lou said, and walked away, giving Freddie a little wave.

Freddie waited until the light turned green and turned right. He circled the block, saw Emmy Lou getting into a car parked a half-block away, and waited. He was two cars behind her when she pulled out of her parking spot.

Chapter Ten

"Look, I'm still shaking," Emmy Lou said, holding out her hands.

"He does have that effect on people."

"I was so scared," Emmy Lou told Karlee. "He wanted to give me a ride. When he got out of his car and walked back to the guy that was blowing his horn, I thought he was going to beat him up."

"What did he say to him?" Karlee asked.

"I couldn't hear. The guy pulled around his car and drove off."

"You didn't give him your phone number, did you?" Karlee asked Emmy Lou.

"Of course not. Do you think I'm some kind of an idiot?"

"I don't know. You gave it to him once before."

"No, I didn't. I never gave him my real number," Emmy Lou said, indignantly.

"Oh. I thought you did. So, then what happened?"

"I just walked away and he drove off."

"So, what were you so afraid of? It's not like he was threatening you."

Emmy Lou shrugged. "I don't know. I guess just running into him was unnerving."

Karlee smiled. "We don't have anything to worry about. Firecracker doesn't know it was us who took his tires. Besides, it was months ago, and he probably forgot all about it while he was in jail. I'm sure he had other things to worry about besides who stole his tires."

"I don't know, Karlee. He never would have gone to jail if we hadn't pulled that prank. I'd still be pretty pissed if it was me."

"Don't worry about it. We'll be fine. You want to go have some lunch?"

"I can't. I'm meeting Mike in a little while."

"Right. You and Mike are back together. How's that going, anyway?" Karlee asked.

"It's good. We have fun and I like him a lot."

"Enough to marry him?" Karlee asked, teasingly.

"I've got to go," Emmy Lou said, ignoring her question. "Call me later?"

"Will do."

Freddie watched Emmy Lou leave the house and get into her car. As soon as Emmy Lou drove away, Freddie pulled up to the front of the house, noted the street number, and drove away. He intended to check out the address on the internet to see who lived there. Was it Emmy Lou or did that house belong to someone else?

"I'm telling you, Karlee, he was parked right down the street from your house," Emmy Lou yelled into her phone. "He must have followed me."

"You sure it was him?"

"Who else around here drives a fucking tank? Of course, I'm sure."

"Calm down. You don't know for sure what he was doing there," Karlee said.

"Really? You don't think he followed me to your house? Do you think that this is all a coincidence? Seriously, Karlee, wake up. I'm in trouble."

"He just wants to date you, not kill you. It looks like he's got the hots for you. Remember, he just got out of jail and probably needs a little nookie."

"Is this a joke to you?" Emmy Lou asked.

"Sorry. I just think you're making too much of this."

"Fine. And, when it's you he's following, tell me how funny you think it is."

"All right. I'm sorry I laughed. You may be right. I guess we should keep our eyes open. After all, there's no way we can miss his truck. We'll know if he's watching us – or you. Right now, it's just you and I still think it's because he has the hots for you."

Emmy Lou let out a deep breath and glanced in her rearview mirror. "Well, I don't see him now, so I guess he stopped following me"

"Quit worrying, will you? And, say hi to Mike for me," Karlee told her.

"Will do. Bye."

"Emmy Lou is on her way," Karlee said when Mike answered his phone.

"Hello to you, too."

"Sorry. I just want to let you know that Emmy Lou is really upset, so don't brush her off thinking she's worrying about nothing."

"What happened?"

"She had a run-in with Firecracker. She thinks he's following her."

"What do you mean a run-in?"

"He saw her walking downtown, stopped, and asked if she wanted a ride. She brushed him off, hoping that was the end of it. Later, when she left my house, she saw his truck parked down the street. She thinks he followed her."

"Shit. She's probably right. Why else would he be

parked there?"

"What do you think is going on?"

"I'm not sure. What I am sure of is that you three opened a can of worms when you stole his tires."

"I know. And, I'm sorry we ever did that. It looks like we may have a problem," Karlee stated.

"You think?"

"Anyway, just let Emmy Lou vent and be nice."

"I'm always nice. I'll talk to you later."

When he found out that the house belonged to Karlee Campanale, Freddie smiled. She has to be Mike Campanale's sister, he thought. That son of a bitch probably put those three women up to stealing my tires. He's such a chicken shit, he can't even do his own dirty work.

He looked up from his phone and motioned to Pistol to bring him another beer. He felt kind of bad that Emmy Lou had been part of it. He had liked her the night he had met her in the bar. Taking care of the Campanale women was gonna be a breeze, but Emmy Lou was going to be a tough one.

Chapter Eleven

"What do you mean, she's missing?" Michael exclaimed. "How the hell could she be missing?"

"She just is," Karlee said, trying not to cry again. "Her bed hasn't been slept in, she hasn't been to work, and no one has seen her for two days. And, her car is in her parking lot."

Mike was silent, taking in what Karlee was telling him. His baby sister had disappeared. "Have you called the police?" he asked.

"They're on their way over now. I'd feel better if you were here, Mike. Can you come over?"

"Of course. I'm on my way. I'm sure everything is okay, Karlee. You know Rebecca. It would be just like her to take off for a couple of days and forget to tell anyone that she was leaving."

"I pray to God you're right, Mike. But I have a bad feeling about this. It has Firecracker written all over it. We've been on needles and pins ever since he started stalking Emmy Lou. Who knows what he's capable of doing? I'm scared, Mike."

"I'll be there in a couple of minutes. Hang in there, kiddo."

Karlee put her phone on the table and sat back, wondering what had happened to Rebecca. She should have known something was wrong when Rebecca hadn't returned her last two calls. She should have called the police earlier.

"You can't keep me here forever, you know," Rebecca told the man. "The police are probably looking for me right now."

The man smiled at her. "Sure I can. I can keep you here as long as I want. I can do anything I want to you and there's nothing you can do about it."

"I'll scream," she said.

The man laughed. "Please do. There's nothing I like better than a screaming woman. It turns me on."

"You're a sick prick, you know that?" Rebecca shouted.

"Oh, my. You hurt my feelings," the man replied, sarcastically. He stood and started walking towards the door.

"Where are you going?" she asked him.

"Why look at you. Missing me already."

"I'm hungry. Get me something to eat."

The man laughed aloud. "You're giving me orders? You'll eat when I tell you."

"I want something from Culvers. Get me a butter burger and a chocolate shake. No fries. And, definitely no onions. And, I have to pee."

"Again? For crying out loud, you just went."

"It's the coffee. It goes right through me."

The man sighed and reached into his pants pocket. He took out a key, bent down, and unlocked the manacle that was around her ankle.

"I don't know why it's necessary to keep me chained. You lock me in when you leave. There are no windows for me to climb out of. How do you think I'm going to escape?"

"I don't trust you," the man told her.

"I'll make you a deal," Rebecca said. "You don't chain me up and I promise not to try to escape."

The man looked at her and grinned. "You really think I'm that stupid?"

Rebecca smiled back at him. "I promise. Seriously, I won't try anything. The bathroom is right there, so I could at least go when you're not here. Please."

The man held her gaze for a couple of seconds and then shook his head back and forth. "I don't think it's a good idea. You'll try something."

"I promise I won't. Pleeeease," she begged.

"Go do your business. I'll think about it for a minute."

Rebecca smiled at him and went into the adjoining bathroom. She closed the door and then stood there looking around the room. She waited a minute, flushed the toilet, and turned on the cold water faucet. A few seconds later, she walked back into the bedroom.

"Well, whataya think?" she asked.

"I don't see any way you're gonna get out of here without a key," the man said. "Okay, no shackles. But, you damn well better not try anything. If you do, I'm gonna tie you by your hands and feet to the bed. Got it?"

"Got it," Rebecca said. "I knew you weren't all bad"

"Ya, right," the man grunted. "I'm leaving. Just behave yourself."

"Don't forget my food," Rebecca replied, smiling her best smile at him.

Detective John Peppers closed his notebook and put it into his jacket pocket. He reached down and picked up a picture of Rebecca that was lying on the coffee table. "I'll take this with me. If you think of anything else, give me a call," he said as he handed

Karlee his card.

"What do you think, Detective? I mean, what are the chances of finding her?"

"It's been over 48 hours," he replied. "You should have called us earlier."

"I thought it had to be at least 48 hours before you cops considered someone missing," Karlee said.

"No. It used to be 24 hours but there's no time limit if there is a real concern that something might have happened. Especially, if that person doesn't have a habit of running off. You know, like kids, who get pissed at their parents and want to make them suffer a little. But you really should have called us immediately. After 48 to 72 hours – well, the chances of finding her. . . ."

"What? The longer it goes, the bigger the chance that she'll be dead? That's right, isn't it?" Karlee interrupted. "That's what you were going to say, weren't you?"

Detective Peppers looked over at Mike Campanale, wondering what was going on in his head. "Is there anything else you can tell me, Mike? You haven't said much and I get the feeling that perhaps more is going on here than what you've told me."

Mike looked questioningly at Karlee. She shrugged, not sure if she should respond.

"All right, guys," Detective Peppers said, "let's hear it. If you want us to find your sister, you need to tell me what's going on."

"Well," Mike started, "we don't have any evidence to go on and we don't want to get anyone in trouble but there is one thing."

Detective Peppers sat back down in the chair and took out his notebook. "It seems that there always is that one thing. Okay, why don't you two start at the beginning?"

Chapter Twelve

"How are you doing, Freddie?" Detective Peppers asked when Freddie opened his front door.

"What can I do for you, Detective?"

"I need to ask you a few questions. Can I come in?"

"I'm on my way out. I have therapy in half an hour," Freddie told him.

"I heard you were shot. How's that shoulder coming along?"

"Fine. Now, if you don't mind, I've got to get ready."

"I'll only be a few minutes. It's important."

Freddie hesitated, wondering if he should talk to Peppers, or any cop for that matter, without an attorney present. He shrugged, stepped back, opened the door a little wider, and motioned for Peppers to come in.

"What's so important?" he asked the Detective.

"I've got a missing person case and your name was mentioned. Time is of the essence, so maybe you can help me out a little here."

"Who's missing?"

"A woman named Rebecca Campanale. Do you know her?"

"Campanale. Hmmm. The name's familiar. Does she have a brother named Mike?"

"She does. Do you know him?"

"He used to be my insurance guy."

"Used to be?"

"Ya. I have a new company that takes care of my insurance needs."

"So, why you'd quit him?" Peppers asked

"The son of a bitch turned off my auto pay while I was incarcerated. He let all my insurance policies lapse, including my health insurance. He didn't tell me about it until after I was shot and in the hospital. That fucker cost me a fortune in medical bills."

"I bet that pissed you off," Peppers commented.

"Damn right it did," Freddie exclaimed.

"Word is that you two had a pretty serious fight a while back. What was that all about?"

"Where did you hear that?" Freddie asked, surprised that the cop knew about the fight.

"Just word on the street. I hear you hurt him pretty bad."

"That's exaggerated. We exchanged a few blows. That's all it was. I just hit him a little harder than he hit me and he had a few bruises the next day."

"What was the fight about?" Peppers asked him.

"Damned if I remember," Freddie answered. "It was a long time ago."

"Could it be that he accidentally spilled a drink on you at the Squirrel House and you got mad? That's what I heard."

"So, did word on the street tell you that, too? Seems like word on the street has a big mouth," Freddie remarked, sarcastically.

"Do you know his sister, Rebecca?" Detective Peppers asked.

"No. I've never met her," Freddie told him.

Peppers reached into his pocket and pulled out a photo and showed it to Freddie. "This is her. Ring any bells?"

"Pretty girl, but no. I don't know her."

"Did you ever meet Karlee Campanale?"

"Can't say I did. I don't know any of Mike's relatives."

"What about friends? Do you know Emmy Lou Larson?"

Freddie looked at the cop, wondering how much he knew. "What about her?"

"Do you know her?" Peppers asked again.

"I do. I met her one night at the Squirrel House. We had a few drinks and we talked. That's it, though. I thought she was nice."

"Did you ever call her or date her?"

"Hell, no. That's the only time I've talked to her."

"So, you didn't see her a few days ago and talk to her. Maybe ask her for her phone number?"

Freddie didn't say anything. He decided it was time to quit being the nice guy and get Peppers out of his house. "I think we're done here, Detective. I've really got to get going."

"Have you been following her, Freddie? Maybe harassing her?"

"What the hell are you talking about? Maybe you should tell me what's going on before I answer any more of your questions. Did something happen to Emmy Lou? I thought you said it was Rebecca Campanale who was missing."

"It is. Where were you Tuesday night?"

"Tuesday night? Let me think a minute. The whole night?"

"Let's say from five o'clock until six the next morning."

"I left work at about seven, went to my mom's house for dinner, and spent the rest of the night getting shit-faced at the Squirrel House. I figure about thirty people can tell you I was there until closing time."

"Did you drive home shit-faced?"

"Nope. Frank took my keys and called me a Uber ride. He gave my keys to the driver and the driver – George was his name - gave them back to me when he dropped me off."

"How can you remember the name of the driver if you were so drunk?"

"I was drunk, not passed out. So, what's this all about?

"If I question Frank and the Uber driver, are they going to tell me the same story?"

"Of course. I have no reason to lie."

"All right, then. I guess that's enough for now."

Detective Peppers headed for the front door, hesitated, and turned to look back at Freddie. "How's that ride of yours?" he asked.

Freddie grinned. "Man, it's the greatest."

"Did you get it fixed?" Peppers asked.

"What do you mean fixed?"

"I heard it got damaged before you went to jail."

Freddie frowned. "Man, do you know everything that goes on around here?"

Peppers laughed. "It's my job to know what's going on."

"I had a couple of tires ripped off. Okay? No damage. Just a lot of aggravation."

"Ever find out who did it?"

Freddie stared at the cop, wondering what he was getting at. "Nope," he finally answered. "I don't have a clue."

Detective Peppers looked Freddie in the eyes and grinned. "Well, Freddie, word on the street is that you do know."

"Goodbye, Detective. And, if you run into word on the street, tell him to go fuck himself."

Freddie turned and walked into the kitchen.

Detective Peppers smiled, opened the door, and left.

Chapter Thirteen

Rebecca knew she was in a basement. After all, how many bedrooms are windowless? She also knew that the house she was in had probably cost an arm and a leg. The room was tastefully decorated and there was no doubt that the furnishings hadn't come cheap.

She checked the closet and, except for a spare pillow and blanket on the top shelf, it was empty. The drawers in the dressers were also empty and the bathroom only had necessities, like soap, towels, and toilet paper. There had been a new toothbrush and toothpaste on the sink's countertop, which she had been using since she had been there.

She needed some shampoo and lotion and made a mental note to tell Dumb Ass to get her some. She smiled, wondering if he would pick up the hamburger and shake that she had ordered. He obviously didn't mind being bossed around. Probably married and used to it, she thought.

All in all, now that she was no longer chained, she was comfortable. She fluffed up her pillows, and lay back on the bed, deciding to watch a little TV. After a few minutes, she picked up the remote and turned it off, not able to concentrate on some program about how lizards mate.

Rebecca knew she should be afraid but she was more pissed off than scared. She had been grabbed as she was getting out of her car in front of her apartment building. The next thing she knew she was waking up on a strange bed, with an absolutely fantastic hunk of a man, sitting in a chair watching her.

Tony had smiled when she looked over at him and said, "Do I know you?"

"That's your question?" he had asked. "Not, where am I? Or, what happened?"

"I know what happened and you sure aren't going to tell me where I am. I'd like to know, though, if you plan on raping or killing me."

He had laughed. "Not yet and not if you behave yourself."

"Why am I here? Ransom? If that's what you're looking for, you're out of luck. My family doesn't have any money, and even if they did, I doubt they would pay to get me back."

"They love you that much, do they?"

"What's your name?"

"You don't need to know."

"Well, I need to call you something."

Tony had looked at her and smiled, and Rebecca had suddenly felt scared. Scared, because her stomach had butterflies and she had felt an attraction to him.

"Okay, then." Rebecca had said, hoping her voice wasn't giving away what she had felt. "Don't tell me. I'll just call you Dumb Ass. How's that?"

"Fine with me," he had replied. "I'm leaving. Do you need to use the bathroom before I go?"

"Where are you going?"

"Do you?"

"Yes," she had answered and then realized, for the first time since coming to, that she was chained.

Rebecca knew she had been in the basement bedroom for over two days. She figured Karlee and Mike would have reported her missing by now and she would be found soon. She might get out of this mess but only if she kept her head and stayed focused.

She had no idea why this was happening. There were only two people that she could think of who might do this. First and foremost, of course, was Freddie Demonti. If he knew she was part of the reason he went to jail, he could be looking for revenge. The other person was Jake, her ex-boyfriend. He hadn't taken it well when she had broken off their engagement a few weeks ago. She figured either one of the men could be angry enough to do this to her, even if it was a little extreme.

Jake was well off and had a nice home but it certainly wasn't the one she was in. She knew his house from top to bottom and there were no bedrooms in his basement. She didn't know about Freddie's home. Besides, Jake would never hire someone to kidnap and scare her. But Freddie Demonti would.

Her stomach growled, reminding her that she hadn't had anything to eat since yesterday. She hoped that Dumb Ass would be back soon with her food. Man, she thought, he sure is sexy. I wonder if I . . . Stop it, she told herself. He's holding you hostage and you're thinking about screwing him. Get your head together, girl or you're really gonna be in trouble.

Tony talked into a drive-up speaker and ordered a hamburger with no onions and a chocolate milkshake. He pulled up, paid the girl working the window, and waited until she handed him the bag that held his order. He drove off, smelling the hamburger as its fumes filled the air.

Chapter Fourteen

It had been five days since Rebecca had disappeared. The police had exhausted every possible lead and the investigation had basically come to a standstill. Mike and Karlee hadn't had a decent night's sleep, were on edge, and were extremely irritable. They had run out of ideas and were constantly snapping at each other.

Detective Peppers had interviewed all of Rebecca's friends but no one knew anything or had any suggestions on what might have happened. People, who lived in her apartment building and had been home at the time of the possible abduction, hadn't seen anything. The interview with her ex-boyfriend yielded no results, as Jake Frolly had been out of Illinois at the time Rebecca disappeared.

No one knew for sure if she was missing, had been kidnapped, or had disappeared on her own.

Rebecca still did not have a clue as to where she was. Three days ago, although it was taped off and considered a possible crime scene, Tony had broken into her apartment. He had retrieved some of her clothes, and other essentials she deemed necessary to be comfortable during her confinement. She had made a list and had told him not to come back if he didn't get every item she wanted.

Now, as she soaked in a bathtub filled with bubbles, she wondered if she was ever going to get out of this room and see her family again. A few days ago, she had hidden behind the door and hit Dumb Ass over the head with a small table lamp as he entered the room, thinking it would knock him out. The blow barely fazed him, and he had grabbed her and thrown her onto the bed, saying if she tried anything else he would chain her up again.

Rebecca jumped as she heard the door to the bedroom open. Dumb Ass had left about a half-hour ago, telling her he would bring her dinner when he returned later in the day. Rebecca didn't move, holding her breath, wondering who had entered the room.

"Well, aren't you the cute package, all clean and naked?" the man said.

Rebecca turned in the tub to see who was talking to her. Her first reaction was fear but anger quickly took over. "Get the hell out of here," she yelled.

The man walked over to the toilet, lowered the seat, and sat down, facing her. "I've waited a while for this, Rebecca," he said. "Because of you and your fucking family, I spent six months of my life in jail."

"Hey, I didn't tell you to beat the shit out of that guy," Rebecca snapped back. "It was your fucking temper that put you in jail. It certainly wasn't me."

"Oh, it was you, all right," Freddie said. "You and that prank with the dildos. You seriously thought that was funny, didn't you?"

Rebecca smirked. "It kinda was," she replied.

"My mother's jaw was broken because of you," Freddie yelled.

"Well, you dumb shit; you're the one who broke it."

"You really are a bitch, aren't you?"

Rebecca stared at him, not responding. She reached for some bubbles at the end of the tub, and pulled them closer, trying to cover her exposed body.

"Get out of the tub," Freddie ordered.

"What? No way. I'm not getting out with you in here. You get out of here first."

"Get out or I'll take you out," Freddie exclaimed.

Rebecca considered her options. She decided she didn't want to be naked and manhandled, so she stood up, glaring at Freddie. She reached for a towel that was hanging on a hook, covered herself, and got out of the tub.

"Satisfied?" she asked.

Freddie grinned. "Drop the towel," he told her.

"Go to hell," she retorted.

Freddie reached over, grabbed the towel away from her, and stared at her body. "Nice," was all he said, and walked out of the room.

Rebecca was totally off balance, not sure what to do next. She dried herself off, put on her robe, and went into the bedroom. Freddie was nowhere to be seen.

Three hours later, Rebecca was under the covers, curled up into a ball, sleeping. She had finally gotten her shaking under control and had drifted off.

Tony unlocked the door and stepped into the room. He looked over at Rebecca and smiled. She looks like a little girl, all tucked in and curled up, he thought. He set the bag with her dinner on a dresser and walked over to the bed.

"Rebecca," he said softly. "I have your dinner."

Rebecca moaned, rolled over, and looked up at him. She reached up and grabbed his hand, pulling it towards her.

"Kiss me," she demanded. "I want you to kiss me."

Tony pulled his hand back, looked down at her,

and saw the need in her eyes. He hesitated, then bent over and touched his lips to hers. She grabbed the front of his shirt and pulled him down onto the bed, next to her. He gathered her into his arms and held her close, kissing her passionately.

"Make love to me," she whispered.

"Rebecca, are you sure this is what you want?" he asked.

"I've never been more sure of anything in my life," she answered.

Tony threw back the blanket that covered her, surprised at her nakedness. "My god, you're so beautiful," he told her, as he stood and hastily shed his clothes. He lay back down beside her, engulfed her in his arms, and kissed her lips. She moaned quietly, as she melted into his body, ready to become one.

When Rebecca came out of the bathroom, Tony was dressed and sitting in the overstuffed chair. He grinned at her. "Wow! That was great."

She smiled. "It was okay."

"Just okay?"

"Would you like me to rate you on a scale of one to ten?"

"Not unless you're gonna give me a ten."

"A ten? Seriously? If I give you a ten, you'll get a big head. I'll give you an eight."

"What the hell? I'm better than an eight."

"You're an eight. Period."

"How about a nine?"

"I think you're gonna have to work a little harder to be a nine," Rebecca said, laughing.

"Woman, I think you're trying to kill me."

"Are you leaving?"

"In a couple of minutes. Your dinner is cold."

"I can heat it up in the microwave. Freddie was here. Did you know that?"

Tony stared at her, obviously surprised. "Did he hurt you?" he finally asked.

"He caught me soaking in the tub. He saw me naked."

"Did he touch you?"

"No. But he scared the crap out of me. When am I gonna get out of here..." She stopped talking and looked at him questioningly.

"What?" he said.

"I don't know your name. I just made love to you and I don't even know your name. I can't keep calling you Dumb Ass now."

He smiled. "My name is Tony."

"I like it. Tony what?"

"Demonti," he told her.

Rebecca stared at him. "No," she said softly. "Please don't tell me you're Freddie's brother."

"Sorry."

"And, this house?"

"It's mine."

Rebecca backed away from him. "Get out," she yelled. "Get out of my sight."

"Please, Rebecca, let me explain. At first, Freddie told me this was a joke and asked if I'd help him out. You were only supposed to be here for a few hours; just long enough to scare you."

Rebecca stared at him as he talked, tears filling her eyes. "So, what happened between us is just part of a joke? Is that what you're telling me?"

"God, no. Please, don't think that. What happened between us was wonderful. I want to take you in my arms right now, and never let you go." Tony took a step towards her, reaching out to her. "I'm sorry. I don't..."

Rebecca held up her hands, stopping him. "How could you do this to me? Just get the hell out. Now!"

"Rebecca, please don't do this. Let me explain. Please."

She turned her back to him, not wanting him to see the tears flowing down her cheeks.

Tony stood still, unsure of what to do. Finally, he turned around and walked out of the room. It wasn't until later that Rebecca realized she hadn't heard the click of the door being locked.

Chapter Fifteen

"What the hell do you mean; you can't tell me where you've been? Are you kidding me?" Karlee screamed at her sister. "Mike and I have been worried sick about you. I haven't slept in over a week thinking that all sorts of horrible things happened to you. And, now you have the guts to sit here and tell me you can't tell me what happened? Well, you sure as hell can and will tell me. Right now, Rebecca! Where have you been?"

Rebecca was sitting in Karlee's kitchen, her backpack on the floor by her feet, looking at the label on a can of pop. "Are you sure you don't have any diet pop? This has sugar in it," she said, holding up a can of Coke.

Karlee stared at her. "Unbelievable," she muttered. "You're worried about a little sugar. Fuck the sugar, sister. Just drink it."

Rebecca wondered if Karlee was ever going to cool off. "Do you think it's okay for me to enter my apartment?" she asked, changing the subject. "I was there and there's police tape on my door and a sticker saying that no one should enter."

"You've been home?"

"I just said I was there."

Karlee picked up her phone and made a call. "I'm calling Mike," she told Rebecca. "Maybe he can get you to tell me where you've been."

"Good. Then, I can tell both of you, at the same time, that I don't know where I was. Maybe you should call the police, too, and ask them to join us," Rebecca snapped.

Karlee looked questioningly at her sister. "What

the hell is going on, Rebecca? Did something bad happen to you?"

Rebecca looked away. "Well, if being kidnapped is something bad – then, yes. I guess it did," she finally said.

Detective John Peppers smiled gently at Rebecca. Karlee had called him about an hour ago, told him that her sister was at her house, and wanted to know if it was okay for Rebecca to go home. He told Karlee to keep Rebecca there until he had a chance to talk to her.

Rebecca smiled back at him, waiting for him to say something.

"How are you doing, Rebecca?" he said, reaching into his pocket. He took out a package of gum and offered her a piece.

"No, thank you. I don't chew gum."

"I just stopped smoking," Peppers said. "This helps."

"Good for you," Rebecca said, indifferently.

"You know we've been worried about you," Peppers said. "I can't tell you how happy I am to see that you're back and in one piece. So, tell me where you were for the five days. It's five, right?" he asked, looking over at Karlee.

"Right," Karlee replied.

Rebecca looked him in the eyes and said, "I don't have any idea where I was."

Peppers sat back in his chair and stared at her. "So, you don't know where you were. Tell me, Rebecca, do you know how you got where you were?"

"Are you asking me if I know how I got wherever it was that I was held?"

"That's right."

"I do know."

"Could you tell me?"

"I was getting out of my car to go into my apartment, and someone grabbed me from behind and threw me into the trunk of their car. The next thing I remember is waking up in a strange house."

"Did you see who grabbed you?" Peppers asked.

"No. And, when I came to, I was shackled to a bed and blindfolded."

"Is that your backpack on the floor there?"

"It is."

"Did you have it with you when you were kidnapped?"

"I did."

"What's in it?" Peppers asked her.

"A change of clothes and some makeup and stuff. Just stuff I use when I go to the gym."

"Do you know where you were in this house? I mean, what room you were in? Could you see outside?"

"No windows. I think I was in a basement."

"What about food and water? Who brought it to you?"

"Detective, let me stop you here. This is how it went. Twice a day there would be a knock on the door. That was the signal for me to put a sack over my head, so I couldn't see. The person would unshackle me and let me use the washroom. Then, I would be shackled again, and the person would leave, locking me in. There would be a bag on the dresser with food for me to eat. When I was alone, I could take the sack off my head."

"What about his voice? Would you recognize it again if you heard it?"

"I think so," Rebecca answered. "I'm pretty sure it was a man but I can't say for positive."

"I see. Was it always the same person who showed up?" Peppers asked her.

"I really can't say. He or she rarely talked. When someone did talk to me, it was always a man. The same man."

"What about your surroundings? You say you think you were in a basement. Except for no windows in the room, why do you think that?"

"Well, for starters, the floor was cement but the walls were paneled. It looked like someone started to finish the room, but didn't complete it. It was pretty chilly but I did have enough blankets to keep me warm. Except for being chained up, I guess you could say I was comfortable enough."

"Did anyone tell you why you were there? I don't get why someone would kidnap you and not ask for a ransom. Did anyone say anything at all?"

Rebecca gave him a sad smile. "That's what's so confusing. I don't understand why I was there. One day I'm dumped in a cold, damp basement and five days later I'm dumped on the street. I haven't got a clue why."

"Your sister mentioned that Freddie Demonti was probably behind this. Why would she think that?"

Rebecca glanced over at Karlee and shrugged her shoulders. "I have no idea. He is the only person I can think of that might have done this but I certainly have no proof of that. I certainly didn't tell her that."

"I think I'll get a search warrant for Freddie Demonti's house. If he has a room in his basement, like what you're describing, I'd like you to take a look. You know, to see if it's where you were held. Would you be open to that, Rebecca?" Peppers asked.

"You think I might have been held in Freddie's house? I don't know. That would be kinda ballsy, don't you think?"

"Well, Freddie certainly has the balls to do something like this," Peppers replied.

"Is there anything else, Detective?" Rebecca asked. "I'd like to go home."

"Of course, you would. We don't need your apartment any longer. You can go home whenever you want."

"Thank you," Rebecca said. "I can't wait to take a shower."

Detective Peppers looked over at Mike, who had been quiet, listening to his sister and the detective converse. "You want to say something, Mike?" he asked.

"I'm not really sure. This whole thing doesn't make any sense to me. Perhaps, after Rebecca has had a chance to clean herself up and relax a little, she'll be a little more helpful."

Mike looked over at Rebecca, wondering what the hell was going on. "You haven't given Detective Peppers much to go on, Rebecca. Are you sure you're okay?"

Rebecca glared at her brother. "I'm fine. I'm sorry if I can't solve the detective's case for him but I can't tell him what I don't know. But you're right about one thing. I need to go home and relax."

Rebecca looked at Detective Peppers. "Do I just remove the tape and sticker from my apartment door? I mean, is it okay to do that?"

Peppers smiled at her. "Of course, it is. Just toss it in the wastebasket. We're done there."

"Thank you," Rebecca said.

"One thing, though, Rebecca," Peppers said.

She sighed, and said, "Yes? What is it?"

"I want you to come down to the station sometime tomorrow and give us a written statement."

"Seriously? Isn't this enough?"

"I'm afraid it isn't."

"Fine. I'll be there sometime in the afternoon."

Peppers reached into his pocket and took out a business card. "Here's my number, if you need to call me," he said and handed her his card.

Chapter Sixteen

Rebecca wasn't in the least bit sorry about lying to her brother and sister. She had already made up her mind not to tell anyone that she had been held in the basement of Tony Demonti's home. Well, at least not until she worked out her feelings about him. On one hand, she would like to see him down on his knees begging her forgiveness. On the other hand, she would like to see him down on his knees with his face in her crotch.

She decided not to mention the fact that it was Firecracker who had her kidnapped. She was sure if she gave the cops that information, Tony's involvement would come out. After all, it was Tony who grabbed her off the street. Did he really think it was a prank? Rebecca doubted it.

Rebecca knew Tony had left the bedroom door unlocked on purpose. He was nowhere to be seen when she had ventured out of the bedroom and up the stairs to the kitchen. Once in the kitchen, she had simply opened the back door and walked out.

She wondered what Firecracker was going to do when he found out she was gone. It was common knowledge that if anyone crossed him there would be hell to pay. She hoped that Tony wouldn't be the recipient of Firecracker's violent temper.

It had come as a total surprise when she found out that Firecracker had a brother. She had lived in Cowtown all her life and had never heard of him. Rebecca started to wonder if he really was Firecracker's brother or if Tony had made that up.

There were too many unanswered questions and Rebecca wanted answers. She needed to get home and work this all out. Her head was telling her that she needed to tell Detective Peppers the truth when she saw him tomorrow. Her heart, on the other hand, wanted to keep Tony safe.

Freddie Demonti was pacing back and forth in Tony's kitchen. He had a beer in one hand and an unlit cigarette in the other.

"You're not thinking about lighting that in here, are you?" Tony asked him.

"Maybe," Freddie said, taking a swig of beer. "I will if I want to."

"No, you won't, Freddie. Smoking is not allowed in my house. You know that."

Freddie threw the cigarette into the kitchen sink. He glared at Tony, obviously upset and looking for a fight. "How the hell could she get out? I don't get it?"

Tony shrugged. "I guess I forgot to lock the door. Anyway, Freddie, enough was enough. What the hell were you keeping her down there for anyway?"

"If she talks to the police, we're both gonna spend a long time in prison. You know that, don't you?"

"Well, if that happens, then I guess we will. And, we deserve it. I don't know what the hell I was thinking, agreeing to grab her. What were your plans, anyway? To keep her there forever?"

"Of course not. I honestly don't know. I just wanted to punish them."

"Them?"

"Ya. Her and her sister. And, that stuck-up broad, Emmy Lou. I didn't think it through, I guess."

"You guess?" Tony exclaimed. "This has to end. You need to forget about those women and what happened. What's done is done."

"I know," Freddie replied. "It's just that I'm so pissed off at them, I can't think of anything else. How can you expect me to let them get away with making a fool out of me?"

"Shit happens. Let it go," Tony told him. "Right now the only thing you should be worried about is a knock on your front door from the cops."

"What about you? You took her, you held her in your house, and you're the one who brought her the food she ate. Hell, I only visited her once. You're the one who's in deep shit trouble here, Bro'."

"And, if you hadn't shown your face, she never would have known that you were behind it all."

"Fuck!" Freddie exclaimed. "This is messed up, man."

"Let's wait and see, Freddie. Right now that's all we can do."

Rebecca had just stepped out of the shower when her phone rang. She picked it up, didn't recognize the number, and refused the call. She dried herself off and slipped into a robe, tying it in the front as she walked to her bed. She pulled back the covers and crawled in between the sheets. She was asleep seconds after her head hit the pillow. The nightmare started a few minutes after that.

She was naked and being chased down a long hall by a huge red and white firecracker that had arms and legs. She came to a big door and pounded on it, hoping that someone would hear her cries for help. The firecracker caught up to her, grabbed her by her arms, and threw her to the floor, forcing her legs apart. As she looked up, the firecracker metamorphosed into a huge penis and started to crawl toward her vagina. She screamed.

Suddenly, the door opened and Tony was standing there. He kicked the penis, which was crawling up Rebecca's legs, into the air, heard it land with a thump, and watched as it slithered away

"You know you want it," he said, gazing down at her, as he unzipped his jeans. She reached for him and pulled him close. His mouth found hers and as he hungrily kissed her, she arched her back and cried out, "Now! Take me now."

Rebecca shuddered, as she orgasmed in her sleep. She was sweating and her heart was racing. She opened her eyes and lay there, still feeling the throbbing between her legs.

Well, that was a first, she thought. But I certainly could have done without the firecracker. She smiled, as she thought of Tony, closed her eyes, and fell back to sleep.

Rebecca didn't hear the phone when it rang the second time.

Chapter Seventeen

"I don't get it," Karlee said to her sister. "If you know for a fact that it was Firecracker that kidnapped you, why won't you tell the police?"

"There are a couple of reasons," Rebecca answered. "First, it's been over two weeks since I told my made-up story, and lying to the police isn't a good thing. It might be obstruction or something and I don't want to have to deal with that. Secondly, Freddie didn't hurt me or anything and we did kinda mess up his life when he went to jail."

"So, you're just gonna forget the whole thing happened? Is that what you're telling me?"

"There's more to it than that, Karlee."

"What more could there be? You spent five days in a cold, damp basement and you're gonna forget about it? That's totally unacceptable, Rebecca."

Rebecca shrugged. "I don't know why you're so upset. I was the one who was kidnapped, not you. Besides, it wasn't a cold damp basement. I lied about that."

Karlee stared at her. "Unfuckingbelievable. What else did you lie about, Rebecca?"

Rebecca grinned. "The guy that took me was tall, dark, and movie star good-looking. I mean really, really good-looking. His eyes were so brown, they were almost black. And, he was nice, Karlee. I'd tell him to do something and he would do it."

Karlee looked shocked. "You have the hots for him!" Rebecca looked away, starting to blush. "You do, don't you? I know you, Rebecca. What the hell happened in that basement or wherever it was you were?"

"Well, it was a basement. But it was a finished basement and quite comfortable. The room where I was kept had plush carpet, expensive furniture, and there was an attached bathroom. The bed was to die for. All in all, it was pretty nice."

Karlee stared at her, shaking her head from side to side. "I don't believe you. Mike and I almost went nuts worrying about you and you talk like you were on vacation somewhere."

Rebecca grinned. "I'm sorry, Karlee, I didn't mean for it to sound like that. All I'm saying is that I wasn't hurt or treated badly. Am I pissed? You bet your sweet ass I am. Do I want to get even with Firecracker? Of course, I do."

"I would be heading to his house with a loaded gun if it had been me," Karlee stated emphatically.

"You and Emmy Lou were gonna be next. I don't know what Firecracker planned to do to you guys but I know he wanted to get even with all three of us. It seems that he didn't even know what he was going to do with me. I don't think he thought it through, so I just sat there for five days while he was trying to figure it all out."

"So, after five days, he just let you go. Just like that? That doesn't make any sense, Rebecca."

"Actually – now don't get mad when I tell you this. Firecracker didn't let me go. The man who was watching me didn't lock the door and I just walked out of his house."

Karlee looked confused while trying to take in what her sister was saying. "You just left? They didn't put you in a car with a bag over your head and drop you off? You walked out of your own volition, which means you know exactly where you were. My god, Rebecca, is anything you told us the truth?"

Rebecca smiled a huge smile. "Oh, ya. That guy was gorgeous. I'm telling you, Karlee, I almost have an orgasm every time I think about him."

Karlee looked her sister in the eyes. "Oh, my god! You little slut. You had sex with him," she exclaimed.

Rebecca laughed. "Now, do you want to help me figure out how we can get even with Firecracker?"

For the first few days after Rebecca had escaped, Freddie was on pins and needles. If he saw a squad car, he drove in the opposite direction. He was eating Tums like they were candy. Now, he was starting to breathe a little easier. He was sure if Rebecca had squealed on him, the cops would have been pounding on his door by now.

Tony, on the other hand, was just plain frustrated. He had tried calling Rebecca dozens of times, only to have his calls rejected. He couldn't get her off his mind and he finally decided to see her face to face. He figured all he had to do was wait for her to show up in her parking lot.

So, when Rebecca drove home after visiting with Karlee and pulled her car into her parking spot, Tony was there. He waited until she approached her front door and unlocked it. Then, he quietly walked up behind her and put his hand over her mouth.

"Don't scream, okay? I just want to talk to you."

Rebecca mumbled something that Tony couldn't understand and opened the door. Tony followed her into her apartment and removed his hand.

75

"Do you enjoy manhandling all women or is it just me?" she asked sarcastically, as she turned to face him.

Tony grabbed her and pulled her towards him, bringing his mouth close to hers. He softly touched her lips with his tongue, teasing her. Rebecca hesitated for only a second. Then, she wrapped her arms around Tony's neck and returned his kiss.

"I gather you've forgiven me," Tony said smiling, two hours later.

Rebecca grinned at him. "I'll forgive anything you do if that's how you say you're sorry."

Tony kissed her softly. "Is there anything else you want to know?"

"How come I've never heard of you? I know you didn't go to school here."

"Same father, different mothers. Tony's my half-brother. While we were growing up, we saw each other almost every year during summer vacation. I lived out west and, after we got older, we stayed in touch but didn't see each other that often. I was offered a job here a few months ago. The money was good, so I took it, bought a house, moved, and here I am."

"Do you know what your brother does for a living?" Rebecca asked.

"Of course, I do. He has a pawn shop in Chicago. I would guess it does well, based on his lifestyle."

"He's also a loan shark. People who live around here hate him, Tony. He's mean. He put my brother in the hospital because he accidentally spilled a drink on him."

Tony sat back and looked at her. "So, is that the reason you did that crap with the tires and dildos and all?"

"We wanted to shame him and it worked. We just didn't know he would beat somebody up at the park and wind up in jail. It was really nice around here for the six months he was gone. People breathed a little easier, knowing your brother wasn't going to lose it for no reason and beat the crap out of them."

"I didn't know about the loan shark stuff he does. Hell, I just went along with him because he told me it was a prank. He made it sound like you guys knew each other. You know, like you were good friends. He said he just wanted to prank you. Hell, you were supposed to be back home in a couple of hours. I'm so sorry, Rebecca. I really am."

"You know this isn't over," Rebecca stated.

Tony looked into her eyes. "What are you planning? Seriously, Rebecca, whatever it is, it's not a good idea."

Rebecca looked away. Tony reached over and turned her face back to him. "Rebecca? Tell me."

"I'm not really sure but I'm working on something. Don't worry about it. It doesn't concern you."

"Sorry, Babe. But after today, everything you do concerns me."

"And, why's that?" Rebecca asked softly.

"You know why," Tony replied, and pulled her close, hugging her. "Promise me one thing," he said.

"What's that?"

"Just don't kill him. Okay?"

Chapter Eighteen

A week later, while having dinner at the Plantation Restaurant with Karlee and Rebecca, Emmy Lou and Mike announced their engagement. It didn't come as a surprise to Mike's sisters, as Mike and Emmy Lou had been dating on and off since high school. Congratulations were exchanged and Karlee ordered a nice bottle of champagne to celebrate the occasion.

Just as Karlee held up her glass and started to give a toast, Rebecca gasped. Karlee stopped talking, her glass in midair, looked over at Rebecca, and asked, "What's wrong?"

Rebecca shook her head, indicating nothing was wrong. "I'm sorry. I guess I'm seeing things," she said, her face a little pale.

"What are you talking about, Rebecca," Mike asked, a little disturbed that Karlee's toast was interrupted.

"I think I just saw Manny Fitzgerald."

"That's impossible. Manny's been dead for years. How many years is it, Karlee? Ten or twelve, at least, isn't it?"

"It's been..." She hesitated, remembering back to when Manny disappeared. "Nine years," She stated factually.

"We don't know for sure he's dead, though," said Rebecca. "They never found a body."

"That's true," Mike said. "But they had enough circumstantial evidence to show that he probably had been murdered. The police found some of his bloody clothes in the trunk of his car, which was parked on the side of the road. The blood on the driver's seat tested positive for Manny. There were also drag marks, probably from his shoes, on the side of the road. The cops figured that someone had dragged his body into the woods."

Rebecca stared at him. "How do you know so much about it?"

"I followed the case. It was big news at the time."

"Maybe he didn't die. Maybe he just disappeared and made it look like a murder," Rebecca said.

"For crying out loud, Rebecca, it wasn't him. He's dead."

Rebecca smiled and said, "You're right. I'm just being silly. Sorry, Mike. Please, Karlee, continue your toast before the champagne goes flat."

"I don't know anyone that I would rather have for a sister than you, Emmy Lou. We've been friends. . . . "

"Seriously, Karlee?" Rebecca interrupted. "Perhaps, you would like to reword that sentence."

Mike and Emmy Lou laughed.

"That might be a good idea. And, please quit interrupting, Rebecca. I'd like to get to bed before it's time to get up to go to work," Mike said.

"Sorry, Rebecca, that came out wrong. Although, I have to say that, right about now, Emmy Lou is looking pretty good for the number one sister spot," Karlee said, teasingly.

"Sorry. Please, start again," Rebecca said.

"Emmy Lou, since the day we met in high school, you've been like a sister to me. Now, you're going to be a real sister, thanks to Mike who made the wisest choice he could make when he asked you to be his wife. Mike, you better know how lucky you are that Emmy Lou has agreed to marry you. You better treat her right, or you'll have me to deal with. Seriously, here's to the both of you. My best friend, Emmy Lou, and Mike, the best brother a girl could ask for. May your blessings be huge and your problems small. Congratulations, to you both. I love you."

"I'll drink to that," Rebecca said, as they all lifted their glasses and drank.

Rebecca set her glass down on the table and excused herself. "I'm heading for the little girls' room. Does anyone need to come with?"

"I'm good," answered Emmy Lou.

"Same here," said Karlee.

"Don't fall in," Mike said, laughing.

Rebecca gave him a look. "Seriously, Mike? What are you? Ten? I'll be right back," she said and walked away.

Rebecca entered the ladies' restroom, looked around at her surroundings, and smiled. Spotless, as usual, she thought. She opened the door to one of the three stalls but before she had a chance to turn around and close the door, a hand clamped over her mouth. Her body went rigid with fright and she tried to scream.

"Shhh. Quiet," a deep voice demanded.

Holding her tight up against him, he pushed her into the stall and closed the door, locking it. He positioned her, so she was facing the wall while keeping his hand over her mouth. He slowly slid his hand up under her skirt, then hesitated when he realized that she wasn't wearing any panties "Lucky me," he whispered. "You decided to go commando tonight."

Rebecca heard him unzip his fly and held her breath. She shook her head from side to side, trying to free his hand from her mouth. She shuddered, as he entered her from behind. It only took a few seconds before he quietly groaned and pulled out. He turned her, so she was facing him.

"Commando, Rebecca?"

She wrapped her arms around his neck and kissed him, grinning. "I knew it was you," she said.

"No you didn't," Tony replied.

"I'd know your scent anywhere. Will I see you later tonight? You owe me one, you know."

"Just one?"

"I've got to get back to my table before someone comes looking for me," Rebecca said, not answering him. "Now get out of here."

Tony kissed her. "I'll see you later."

Rebecca closed the door after him, sat down on the john, and smiled, thinking she might just owe Firecracker a favor for having kidnapped her.

"Took you long enough," Karlee said, as Rebecca approached their table and sat down.

"I didn't know there was a time limit on peeing. Did I miss anything while I was gone?" Rebecca asked, smiling.

"We were just talking about the wedding," Emma Lou said.

"Have you set a date?" Rebecca asked.

"It will probably be next year sometime. We're thinking about an autumn wedding when it won't be so hot."

"Nice," Rebecca said. "I love fall weddings."

"I want you for a bridesmaid..." Emmy Lou stopped talking when she heard a popping noise and looked over at Mike. "Those were shots," she exclaimed.

"Get down. Everyone, get down," he yelled, as he pulled Emmy Lou down next to him. He glanced over at an elderly couple, sitting a couple of tables away from him, and yelled again. "Get down. Someone's shooting. Get under your table."

The couple stared at him, afraid and unable to move. As Mike ran over to their table to help them, the man's head jerked backward and he went limp.

"Get down," Mike yelled at the woman.

"My husband's been shot," she screamed. "Please. Someone help him."

Mike turned and looked at Emmy Lou as his face registered surprise, and he collapsed.

Emmy Lou had been sedated and was sleeping on Karlee's couch. Rebecca and Karlee sat in silence, trying to comprehend the fact that their brother had been shot right in front of their eyes.

"Emmy Lou really lost it when the doctor told us to go home," Rebecca finally said, breaking the silence.

"I know. She didn't want to leave Mike's side. The doctor was right, you know. We all need some rest. It's been a long night."

"Do you think Mom's okay? She didn't say much at the hospital," said Rebecca.

"She'll be okay. She's strong and Dad will take care of her."

"Actually," Rebecca stated, "when you come right down to it, she'll be the one who will take care of Dad. He was close to falling apart there for a while tonight. I'm really worried, Karlee. Do you think Mike will be okay?"

"Mike will be fine. He just needs to get through the night without any setbacks. The doctor said the next twenty-four to forty-eight hours are critical."

"A friggin' prayer or two wouldn't hurt," Rebecca said.

"I haven't stopped praying," Karlee replied.

"Good."

"You want a drink?" Karlee asked her sister.

"Bourbon, if you have it. Neat."

"No bourbon. I have beer, vodka, and rum. Pick one."

"Got any coke?"

"Diet."

"That's good. Make mine a rum and coke," Rebecca said.

"What do we do now?" Karlee asked, tears starting to roll down her cheeks.

"First, we make sure our brother is okay. Then, we get our fucking revenge," Rebecca angrily replied.

"Firecracker?"

"Who else could it be?"

Chapter Nineteen

"I'm telling you; it wasn't me," Freddie yelled. "I promised you I'd leave it alone, and I have."

"Why don't I believe you, Freddie?" Tony said. "I know you well enough to know you don't put things behind you until you've gotten even."

"Tony. Listen to me. I. Did. Not. Do. This," Freddie said, emphatically.

"Maybe you didn't pull the trigger but that doesn't mean you weren't behind this. You could have hired someone to kill Mike Campanale and those women. You certainly aren't a stranger to violence."

"What the hell does that mean?" Freddie said, raising his voice.

"I hear things, Freddie. You're no angel, beating up people and breaking kneecaps just because they can't pay you on time. Does your mother even know what you do for a living?"

"Don't you mention my mother, you hear? I have a legitimate business. You don't know what you're talking about."

"Are you going to stand there and tell me that you're not a fucking loan shark?"

Freddie stayed quiet, as he stared out Tony's kitchen window. "I help friends out from time to time," he finally said. "Every so often, people get in trouble and they come to me for help. I'm doing a good thing."

"You charge exorbitant interest rates and have your goons kick the shit out of the idiots, who borrow money from you when they can't pay on time. I can't see how that's a good thing. People around here are scared to death of you. You're probably the most hated man in town."

Freddie smirked. "And, probably the richest."

Tony shook his head in disgust. "I want you to stay away from those three women, Freddie. I mean it."

"You don't tell me what to do, Tony. Don't forget that. But you are my brother and I respect you and I'm telling you the truth here. I had nothing to do with that shooting. I'm sorry that Mike Campanale got shot. And, I'm sorry that old guy died - whatever his name was."

Tony looked at Freddie, trying to decide if he could believe him or not. "Right now, I don't know what to believe. Just promise me that you'll leave those women alone. Okay?"

Freddie grinned. "Hell, Bro', I already did but I'll promise again if that will make you feel better." He held up his hand, as if to take an oath, and said, "I promise you that I will leave those three women alone and never, never try to get even for what they did to me. Even though they have it coming," he ended, laughing at the annoyed look on Tony's face.

Detective John Peppers picked up the cup and took a sip of coffee. "This is an excellent cup of coffee. What brand do you use?" he asked Karlee.

"It's called Morning Kiss Coffee. You can't buy it in the stores. I order it on the internet."

"It's very smooth," he said, taking another sip. "I know you have a lot to attend to, Karlee, but I wonder if you remembered anything else about the other night."

She shook her head. "Not really. We were enjoying our dinner. Mike and Emmy Lou had just announced their engagement, we were toasting them, and the shooting started. Mike got up to help the elderly couple at the table next to ours, and both he and the old man got shot."

Karlee choked up and her eyes filled with tears. "I'm sorry. It's just that I can still see the look on Mike's face when he was shot. It's hard to talk about."

Peppers reached over to a box of tissues, pulled a couple out of the box, and handed them to her.

"Thank you," Karlee said, taking the tissues from him. She wiped her eyes, took a deep breath, and gave him a faint smile. "Is there anything else, Detective?"

"I really am sorry to bother you. It's just that we like to get as much information as we can, while it's still fresh in people's minds."

"You're not bothering me. By the way, what was the name of the man that was shot? I feel so sorry for his wife. That was his wife, wasn't it?"

"It was. His name was Arthur Fitzgerald. He was a real badass back in his day."

Karlee's face registered surprise. "Are you sure? I'm sorry. Of course, you're sure."

"Did you know him? You seem surprised."

"No. It's not that. Of course, I've heard of him. Anyone growing up in Cowtown knew about him. My parents and their friends were always talking about Artie Fitzgerald." Karlee sat back on the couch and smiled.

"What?" Peppers inquired.

"When we were little kids, just mentioning him was one of the ways that our parents used to keep us in line. 'You be good or we'll call Artie to come and get you,' they'd say."

"Did it work?" Peppers asked her.

"It did," Karlee said. "Just the mention of his

name and we went from being little brats to little angels in seconds. But that isn't why I was surprised."

"So, what was it?"

"Rebecca thought she saw Manny Fitzgerald while we were at the restaurant. We all told her she was seeing things. Now, I wonder."

"Manny Fitzgerald? He's been dead for years."

"Nine. He's been dead for nine years. Although, right now I'm not so sure."

"Oh, he's dead. No one could lose that much blood and live."

"I guess. But, don't you think it's strange that Rebecca thinks she sees Manny, and a few minutes later his father is shot?"

Detective Peppers picked up his cup and drank the rest of his coffee. He glanced over at Karlee and smiled. "I could sure go for another cup of coffee if there's any left."

"I'll get it."

"Stay there. I'll get it," Peppers said.

As he walked towards the kitchen, Karlee asked, "So, do you think this was a random shooting?"

Detective Peppers brought the coffee pot into the living room and refilled the two cups. "Looks like that's the end of the pot," he commented.

"So, do you?" Karlee asked.

"Think it was a random shooting? No. I don't."

Karlee stared at Peppers. "You think someone was trying to kill Mike?"

"I don't know. Perhaps."

"Or, do you think someone shot Fitzgerald on purpose and that Mike was just at the wrong place at the wrong time? Is that it?"

"Karlee, at this point we're not sure."

Karlee stared at him. "My god! You think someone was trying to kill one of us, don't you?"

"We don't know, Karlee. We're just a day into the investigation. Don't jump to conclusions."

Karlee slumped back on the couch and looked at Peppers. "Do you think it was Firecracker?" she quietly asked.

"Do you?" he responded.

"I did. Now, I'm not so sure." She sighed deeply. "I'm not thinking straight, Detective. I seriously don't know what to think."

Peppers smiled at her. "You've been through a lot these past few weeks, Karlee. You know, with Rebecca being kidnapped and now this with Mike. This probably isn't a good time to bring this up but I'd like you to think about something."

She looked up at him, wondering what was coming next. "What's that, Detective?"

"Please, call me John. So, I was wondering – perhaps – well. . . ."

"What is it?"

"Sorry. Let me start again. Perhaps, when all this is over and you're feeling up to it – well, I was wondering if you'd like to have a cup of coffee with me? You know, just talk a little and..." Peppers stopped talking, embarrassed. "That was foolish of me and totally out of line. Please, forget I said anything."

Karlee looked at him, really seeing him for the first time. He was an extremely good-looking man, with auburn hair and green eyes. He had a good build and was a little on the stocky side. She figured he was somewhere between her age and her father's age. She smiled at him.

"You're right, Detective. I mean, John. That was out of line. But right now, I'd don't want to deal with what is normal. So, thank you, but no. I don't want to have a cup of coffee with you sometime. That's what we're doing right now.

"I'm sorry. I don't know what came over me."

"However, I'd love to have dinner with you. Maybe in a week or two, after things start to settle down."

Peppers grinned. "Really?"

Karlee smiled back at him. "Really. Now, I've got things to do, if you don't mind."

Peppers stood up, reached out, and shook her hand. "I'll wait for you to call me. Of course, there's always the possibility that I'll be talking to you again before that."

Peppers stood there, still shaking her hand. Karlee looked at him. "Can I have my hand back, John? Or, are you planning on taking it with you?"

Chapter Twenty

The explosion came at three o'clock in the morning, blowing out the front windows of Freddie's house and setting his living room on fire.

Freddie, who had just turned out his bedroom light and crawled into bed after a long night of heavy drinking, jumped out of bed and ran down the stairs. When he saw the fire, he hesitated, trying to decide if he should get the hell out of the house or go for the fire extinguisher that was in the kitchen. He went for the extinguisher and managed to put out the fire.

He sat down on his couch, looked around at the damage that had been done to his house, and decided it wasn't all that bad. There were a couple of broken windows, and a chair that matched the couch had been slightly burned. The carpet, where the fire had started, had gotten the worst of it.

A couple of minutes more and I would have been asleep, Freddie thought. As the realization that he could have been burned to death sunk in, Freddie got more and more upset.

The sound of sirens approaching his house brought him to his feet. Figuring someone had heard the explosion and called 911, he walked to the front door and opened it. As a firetruck pulled into his driveway, he noticed a piece of paper taped to the outside of his front door. He pulled it off and read it. "Damn fuckers," he muttered to himself.

"Mr. Demonti?" a voice called to him.

Freddie glanced up and saw a fireman walking toward him. "I'm Demonti."

"Is everything okay? We got a call that there had been an explosion here."

"Everything's fine. I didn't call you."

"Are you saying there wasn't an explosion?"

"As I said, everything is fine here," Freddie answered.

"May I ask how those windows got broken?" the fireman asked, pointing to the broken windows.

"Probably just kids," Freddie replied

"Mr. Demonti, may we go inside? I'd like to take a look around, just to make sure everything is okay."

"There's no need. I'm going to get the windows fixed in the morning."

"Well, I still need to take a look."

The fireman brushed past Freddie and walked into the house.

"Hey, you can't just go in there without..." Freddie quit talking as the fireman stopped in the doorway of the living room and looked around.

"Just what exactly happened here, Mr. Demonti?"

Freddie sighed. "How the fuck should I know? One minute I'm in bed and, the next thing I know, my house is on fire."

"What time did this happen?"

"It was around three o'clock. I heard a crash and an explosion and I ran downstairs to see what had happened. When I saw the fire, I grabbed the fire extinguisher and put it out."

"You were still awake at that time?"

"I had just gone to bed. I'd been out and I didn't get home until around 2:30 or so."

"Did you piss anyone off this evening?"

Freddie gave him a dirty look. "No, Captain, I

didn't."

"We all know it happens from time to time. And, it's..."

"You know what happens?" Freddie interrupted.

"That you piss people off, Mr. Demonti. I'm sorry if that insults you but it's true."

Freddie's clenched his fists, ready to strike out at the fireman.

The fireman glanced down at Freddie's hands and took a step back. "Don't even think about it," he told Freddie.

Freddie's hands relaxed slightly and he shrugged. "Don't worry. I'm not gonna do anything. I'm just pissed off and tired of this kind of crap happening all the time."

"So, you've had other incidences like this?" the fireman asked.

"A few. This is more close up and personal, though."

"I'm going to have to file a report with the police department. Perhaps, you'd like to put some pants on. We're gonna be here for a while."

"What the fuck for? I'm not pressing charges against anyone."

"Someone called us about an explosion and gave us your address. You tried to hide it. A crime has been committed and we need to get to the bottom of it, even if that's not what you want."

"Can't you just leave?" Freddie asked. "I'm tired and I want to get some sleep. I put the fire out, and there's no danger lurking behind closed doors. Let's just drop this. Alright?"

"Sorry. No can do," the Captain said.

Freddie sat down on his couch and stared at the

Captain. "Fine. Do your thing but I'm done talking."

"I'll be right back," the Captain said. "I need to get some things out of the truck. It might be a good idea if you put some pants on before your house is crawling with cops."

Freddie looked down at his crotch and grinned. "I totally forgot I was hanging free."

"Just put some pants on, will you?"

Two hours later, Freddie's house was clear of firemen and cops. The pieces of the incendiary device, which had been thrown through his living room window, had been tagged and bagged. The cops doubted that they would get fingerprints good enough to use. There was little chance this would be solved, so 'don't hold your breath, the police told him.

The police had looked at Freddie's security videos, which had been recorded from the front and back doors but considered them useless. "You really should get a different security system," one cop had stated. "What you've got now is shit, cutting in and out all the time. There is even one section of the video that went totally black."

Freddie's ears had perked up when he heard that comment. The three bitches did this, he immediately thought. But, then, remembering the note that had been taped to his front door, he couldn't be sure.

What Freddie didn't share with the cops was that he had a second security system. The camera was hidden in a big tree in his front yard. Hopefully, the video from that would give him the answers he needed.

He made a pot of coffee, sat down in front of the monitor, and picked up the remote.

Chapter Twenty-one

"What?" Freddie yelled as he opened his front door. "Oh, it's you. What now?"

"I just want to give you an update on our investigation," Detective Peppers said. "Mind if I come in?"

Freddie stepped back to make room for Peppers to enter, motioning for him to go into the living room. "Which investigation?"

"You have more than one going on?" Peppers asked.

"I think so if you count the one from last night."

"What happened last night?"

"Someone tried to burn my house down, with me in it."

Detective Peppers looked surprised. "I hadn't heard about that. Of course, it's early, yet."

"You think?" Freddie said, sarcastically. "It's nine in the morning and I haven't been to bed. Which is exactly what I plan on doing as soon as you leave. So update me and get out of here, would ya?"

"Rough night, huh?"

"You could say that."

"I'm trying to make a connection between you and Artie Fitzgerald. Did you ever do business with him?"

"Old man Fitzgerald? Hell, no. He's way before my time. Why?"

"The bullets removed from Artie Fitzgerald and Mike Campanale match the bullet that the doctor took out of your shoulder. It looks like the same person shot all three of you."

Freddie looked perplexed, trying to take in what

Peppers was saying. "I can't think of any connection. I knew his kid, Manny, when we were younger but he's been dead for years now."

"Did you and Manny ever do business together?"

Freddie looked at him, wondering what he was getting at. "I knew him in high school, Detective. Not much business going on back then."

"When was the last time you saw Manny?"

"How the hell should I know? It might have been a couple of years before he disappeared or it could have been a couple of weeks. I don't remember," Freddie replied. "Besides, you don't know it was the same person. You only know the shots came from the same gun. Anybody could have fired those shots."

"That's true," Peppers agreed. "But most likely it was the same person."

Freddie yawned. "Is there anything else, Detective? I've got to get some sleep."

"That's about it." Peppers walked towards the front door. "Call me if you think of anything." He hesitated and turned back towards Freddie. "Do you have any idea who might have torched your house?"

Freddie snorted. "Not a clue. Probably kids."

"Well, you do piss off a lot of people, Freddie. Maybe you should start being nicer," Peppers said, grinning.

"Maybe people should try being nicer to me. It works both ways, you know."

"I guess. Anyway, call me if you think of anything."

"Sure thing," Freddie told him and closed his front door.

"I hate to tell you this, but I think you're crazy," Karlee said. "What if you'd been caught?"

"Well, I wasn't. I made sure of that."

"Do you understand what you did? You tried to kill a man, for god's sake."

"I would have, too, if someone hadn't called the fire department."

"Let me see if I've got this right. You drive to Firecracker's house in the middle of the night, you're dressed in dark clothes, and you sneak up to his front door hoping no one sees you. Then, you block the security camera and tape a note to his front door. Am I right, so far?" Karlee looked at her, waiting for her response.

"Right."

"Next, you threw a bomb through a window, hoping to set his house on fire and burn him alive. Is that right?" Karlee asked.

"Sounds about right. So?"

"Oh, I don't know," Karlee replied, obviously annoyed. "These are not the actions of a sane person. I just can't understand what you were thinking."

"I was thinking that I wanted to burn down Firecracker's house, with him in it."

"I hope no one saw you. At least it was dark, and you weren't there that long. What do you think? Two or three minutes?"

"Well, not really."

"What do you mean, not really?" Karlee asked.

"I waited in my car for a while. I wanted to see the fire."

Karlee looked at her and shook her head. "You wanted to see him burn to death?"

"Right. But when I heard the firetrucks coming, I left."

"How long did you sit there, watching his house?"

"Maybe five minutes or so. That's what I don't understand, Karlee. How did the firetrucks get there so fast?"

"That's your concern? Here's what you should be concerned about. You were probably caught on camera walking up to his house. Most likely, you were seen parked near his house. Someone might have seen you sitting in your car. But it's damn obvious that someone did see you throw the bomb and called the fire department."

"It wasn't a bomb."

"It wasn't?" Karlee asked. "Then, what the hell was it?"

"Just a few things I threw together."

Karlee looked at her, wondering if she was that stupid. "It fucking exploded! You tried to kill someone! If they recognize you on those security videos, you could spend the next twenty years in prison."

"No one saw my face. I was wearing a mask. Besides, the note I left made it look like whoever did it was someone who owes Firecracker money."

"About that note you left," Karlee said quietly. "Please don't tell me that your fingerprints are on it."

"They might be. But I've never been fingerprinted, so there's nothing to compare them to. Don't worry about it, Karlee. Nothing's going to happen."

Karlee's opened her mouth as if she was going to say something. She closed it and sat back in her chair. "You are unbelievable. I need a drink."

"Seriously? It's only nine o'clock. Don't you think

it's a little early to start drinking?"

"No. Actually, I wish I had started earlier," Karlee replied.

"I've got to go. Remember, you promised me you wouldn't say anything. This is our secret, Karlee. You promised."

"Promise me you won't try anything else," Karlee replied.

"I can't do that. I wish I could, but I can't. Because, Karlee, one way or the other, I'm going to kill Freddie Demonti."

"You're crazy. You know that?"

"Maybe, I am. At this point, I don't care."

Freddie walked back to his kitchen and poured himself another cup of coffee He turned on the video, which had been taken from the camera in the tree. He stopped it when he saw a figure crouching down in the bushes on the side of his house. He studied it, trying to make out a face. He zoomed in and realized the face was covered with some type of mask.

He watched the person cover his front door security camera with a cloth and back away from the door. Then, the person threw a package through the window, grabbed the cloth off the camera, and ran towards the street.

He runs like a girl, Freddie thought to himself. He continued watching until the figure was out of the range of the camera.

He switched over to the video the police had looked at, wondering if he could see anyone on the street or near the front of his house.

After a few minutes, he switched off the monitor,

sat back, and smiled. Gotcha!

Chapter Twenty-two

"It wasn't me," Rebecca yelled.

"If it wasn't you, who was it?" Tony yelled back at her.

"Screw you, Tony! I don't give a rat's ass if you believe me or not. Get the hell out of my house. We're through."

Tony looked shocked. He sat back and took a deep breath. "You don't mean that."

"The hell I don't," Rebecca retorted. "I'm not going to be with someone who doesn't believe me when I tell them something."

"Alright. I believe you. I'm sorry, Rebecca. Really, I am." Tony held out his arms to her. "Come over here and give me a kiss."

"Screw you."

"After you give me a kiss," Tony replied, smiling.

Rebecca gave him a disgusted look. "You don't believe me, do you?"

"Actually, I do. I figure if it had been you who tried to kill Freddie, you wouldn't have gotten so mad. You might have denied it but you're really pissed at me. I really am sorry. Now get over here."

"Please," Rebecca said, grinning.

"What?"

"Say please."

Tony grinned back at her. "Please," he said softly. "Please come over here and kiss me."

Rebecca stayed where she was. She smiled and murmured, "What's in it for me?"

Tony got off the couch, walked over to her, and swept her up into his arms. Rebecca squealed and threw her arms around his neck, laughing as he carried her into the bedroom and threw her down onto the bed.

"Still wondering what's in it for you?" Tony said as he pulled his shirt off.

Rebecca stared at him, amazed at the effect he had on her. She grinned when he pulled off his jeans and tossed them aside.

"Not in the least," she exclaimed.

Rebecca stood by the sink, watching Tony as he sipped his second cup of coffee. Seeing him sitting there, dressed only in his jeans, gave her stomach butterflies. I think I'm falling in love with him, she thought. And, that is probably not a good thing.

"So?" Tony said.

Rebecca realized he was talking to her and she had no idea what he had just said. "Sorry, Babe, my mind was somewhere else. What did you say?"

Tony smiled at her. "Thinking about round two, are you?"

"Not on your life. It's going to take an hour just for my legs to get back to normal."

"I asked how long you plan on keeping us a secret from your family. I don't see what the big deal is if they know we're seeing each other."

Rebecca looked at him like he was crazy. "Seriously? You don't know what the big deal is? My family thinks your brother shot Mike. They would go nuts if they knew about us."

"It wasn't Freddie, Rebecca. He swears he didn't do it and I believe him," Tony said.

"Well, I think he did it. And, so do Mike and Karlee. Even my parents think he did it. I don't think the name Demonti is very popular with the Campanale family right now. I think we should wait until all this crap is sorted out before we tell anyone about us."

Tony sighed. "I see your point. But I certainly had nothing do it with any of this."

Rebecca stared at him, wondering if he was serious. "You're kidding. Right? You kidnapped me. You certainly did have something to do with all of this."

"But you're the only one that knows that. And, look how well it turned out. If I hadn't done Freddie a favor, we would never have met. Just look at all the great sex you would have missed out on. Actually, your family should be thanking Freddie for saving you from being an old maid."

Rebecca drew in a deep breath, shocked at what she had just heard. Tony locked eyes with her and grinned.

"What do you say, Rebecca? Will you marry me?"

Rebecca pulled out a chair and sat down. "What the hell, Tony? Are you crazy? No, I won't marry you. I hardly know you."

"I'd say you know me pretty well."

"I know your body but that certainly doesn't justify marrying you."

"What do you want to know? Just ask and I'll tell you anything."

"You want some more coffee?" she asked, trying to change the subject.

"That's an easy one. No, thank you. I've had my limit for the day. Anything else you want to know?"

Rebecca walked over to the refrigerator and opened it. She stood there, staring at the shelves. Tony was quiet as he watched her. She turned and looked at him, a big grin on her face. "I do believe that what I see is what I'll get. My family will just have to learn to live with it."

Tony looked surprised. "Are you saying yes? Don't play with me, Rebecca."

"I love you, Tony. That's all that's important. So, yes. I'll marry you."

Tony reached out for her hand and pulled her onto his lap. "I love you, Rebecca."

"My legs have stopped shaking," she told him, grinning.

Chapter Twenty-three

Victor Campanale watched as his wife, Cecelia, placed a platter on the table. She handed him a carving knife and took her place at the other end of the table.

"It's so nice to have all my children here at the same time. I can't remember when we were all together for a Sunday dinner," Mrs. Campanale commented.

"It has been a while, hasn't it?" said Mike.

"It wasn't that long ago," Rebecca remarked. "We all had dinner together the week before you were shot, Mike."

"That's right. I forgot."

"Rebecca, would you like to say grace?" Cecelia asked her youngest daughter.

Rebecca turned her head and looked at her mother. "Not really. I didn't know it was my turn. I don't have anything prepared."

Karlee grinned and glanced at Mike.

Mr. Campanale looked at Rebecca. "Just say grace, please."

"Grace," she said, making Mike and Karlee laugh.

"Oh, for crying out loud," Mrs. Campanale exclaimed. "I'll say the blessing."

"No. You will not. Rebecca is going to say grace today. Let's all be quiet, while she racks her brain trying to think of how to thank God for this food we are about to eat," Mr. Campanale told his wife.

Rebecca looked at her father, wondering if she should push him any further. She glanced over at her sister, who was holding back a laugh, and grinned.

"Is something funny, Rebecca?" her father asked.

"Will somebody please say a prayer?" said Mrs.

Campanale. "I didn't spend half the day in the kitchen to sit here and watch our dinner get cold."

"I've got it," Rebecca said. She bowed her head, closed her eyes, and loudly exclaimed, "good food; good meat; good God; let's eat."

Mr. Campanale's head jerked up, he opened his eyes and stared at his daughter. Then, he grinned. "Works for me. Who wants an end cut?"

"That was terrible, Rebecca. Shame on you," said Mrs. Campanale.

"Sorry, Mom."

"Have you and Emmy Lou set a date?" Mrs. Campanale asked Mike, as she passed him the mashed potatoes.

"I'll take the end cut, Dad," Mike said. He looked at his mom and replied, "Next year in the fall sometime. We don't have a definite date yet."

"Well, you better get on it. All the good banquet halls will be booked if you wait much longer," his mother told him.

"We don't need a banquet hall. Emmy Lou and I have decided not to have a large wedding," Mike told her.

"Why, that's just crazy, Mike. All girls want a big wedding with all the trimmings. Are you sure that's what Emmy Lou wants?"

"Emmy Lou and I hardly talked about anything else while I was recuperating in the hospital. We're both sure that's what we want, Mom. Believe me, if Emmy Lou wanted a big wedding, that's what she'd get. But she doesn't and I'm going along with her wishes."

"Then why the long wait if you're not going to have a big wedding, Mike? Why not just get married now and get it over with?" Karlee asked. "Look at all the money you'd save."

"Emmy Lou is moving in with me when her lease is up, which is only six weeks from now. We'll be saving a lot when she isn't paying rent on that apartment of hers."

"Why doesn't she sub-let?" Karlee asked him.

"Not worth the effort for only six weeks," Mike replied.

"You are planning to get married before she moves in with you, aren't you?" Mrs. Campanale asked.

"No, Mom, we're not. I just said we are thinking of a fall wedding next year," Mike replied.

"Well, you better get married before she moves in with you. I don't want a son of mine living with a woman he's not married to."

"Don't worry, Mom. We will each have our own bedroom. Nothing is going to happen."

Mike's mother thought for a few seconds about what he had just said. She smiled at her son. "Alright, then. As long as you have separate bedrooms, I guess it's okay."

Victor Campanale rolled his eyes and wondered how his wife was still so naïve. Yet, it was one of the things he loved about her.

"So, Karlee, what about you? Are you seeing anyone?" her dad asked.

Karlee smiled. "Perhaps."

"What do you mean, perhaps? Either you are or you aren't," her dad said.

"Do you remember Detective Peppers?"

Rebecca's right hand, holding a fork full of potatoes, stopped halfway to her mouth. She looked across the table at her sister, meeting her gaze. "What about him?" Rebecca asked.

"We've gone out a few times."

"Are you serious? You're dating a cop?" Mike asked.

"I sure am," Karlee answered.

"Is it ethical for a cop to date the sister of a person who's been shot? I mean, isn't there an open investigation going on?" Rebecca asked, obviously getting upset. "I mean – well, somehow that just doesn't seem right to me."

Karlee gave her sister a dirty look. "John and I don't think there's anything wrong with it," she replied. "And, we've only had a couple of dates. Really, Rebecca, when did you get so concerned about who I date?"

"Well, I think it's nice that you're seeing someone. We met him when Rebecca was missing and he was very nice. He seems a little old for you, Karlee, but nice," said Mrs. Campanale. "Is everyone ready for dessert?"

"He's not that much older," Karlee said, defensively.

Mr. Campanale looked over at Karlee and asked, "How much older are we talking about?"

"I don't know, Dad. I've never asked him how old he is. Maybe five or six years."

"How about fifteen or twenty?" Rebecca said, sarcastically.

"He is not," Karlee stated emphatically. "You don't know what you're talking about, Rebecca. Anyway, at least I didn't crawl into bed with him before I knew his name, like some people I know."

"Dessert sounds good to me. What did you make, Mom? Please, tell me it's apple pie," said Mike, hoping to get off the subject before his two sisters got into it.

"What about you, Rebecca?" Mr. Campanale said before his wife could answer Mike. "You dating anyone we know?"

Mike groaned and shot his father a dirty look.

"What's your problem?" his dad asked.

"No problem, Dad. Sorry. Let's just get off this subject, okay?"

"Well, I just wondered. That's all," Mr. Campanale said.

Rebecca sat straight up in her chair, looked at her father, and smiled. "I'm so glad you asked me that, Dad," she said. "Actually, there is someone. I was hoping he would be able to come with me today, so you could all meet him, but it didn't work out."

"Oh, Rebecca, that's wonderful," Mrs. Campanale exclaimed.

Karlee looked at her sister and, ever so slightly, shook her head no. Rebecca grinned and shook her head yes. Karlee rolled her eyes and shook her head no again.

"Who is it, Rebecca?" Mike said.

"You don't know him. He didn't grow up in Cowtown and he just recently moved here."

"Well, would you mind telling us his name? He does have a name, doesn't he?" her mother asked.

"Of course, he does," Rebecca said.

Rebecca's family all stared at her, waiting for her answer.

"Oh, ya. One more thing. We're gonna get married. I'm engaged," Rebecca told her family.

Rebecca's father yelled, "What the hell are you talking about, Rebecca? You're gonna marry a man we've never even met?"

Karlee's mouth dropped open. She looked at Rebecca and silently mouthed the words, "Are you nuts?"

Rebecca shrugged her shoulders and smiled as she mouthed back, "Maybe."

Mike looked confused and said, "Wait a minute. Did you just say that you're getting married? Are you pregnant? You are, aren't you?"

Mrs. Campanale teared up. "First Mike and now Rebecca. I'm so happy for you, Rebecca."

Rebecca took a deep breath and let it out. "I know this is sudden and I'm sorry I sprung it on you like this. But I'm sure you're going to love him as much as I do, once you get to know him. And, no, Mike, you ass, I'm not pregnant."

"Please, dear, don't swear," Mrs. Campanale said.

Mr. Campanale sat back in his chair and stared at his youngest daughter. "You still haven't told us his name."

Rebecca hesitated. "Well, the thing is, Dad. Now don't get upset until you hear the whole story."

"Rebecca, just tell me his fucking name!"

"Victor, please don't use that word," Mrs. Campanale remarked.

"Rebecca!" he yelled, ignoring his wife's comment.

"His name is Tony. Tony Demonti."

If someone had dropped a pin, the noise would have made everyone jump. Perhaps, I should have waited, Rebecca thought, waiting for her family to erupt in anger, as her news sunk in. But, no one said a word. They just stared at her.

Finally, Rebecca picked up her glass and took a

sip of wine. "So, how about that dessert?"

An hour later, Rebecca and Karlee thanked their parents for a delicious meal, kissed them goodbye, and walked down the driveway to their cars. Karlee grabbed Rebecca's arm and pulled her towards her.

"What now, Karlee? I'm done having this conversation."

"I can't believe you didn't tell me about you and Tony."

"I did. I just didn't tell you his name."

"Rebecca, do you have any idea what you've gotten yourself into? He kidnapped you for god's sake. He's no better than his no-good brother."

"Stop. I don't want to talk about it."

"I'll never understand what makes you tick."

"Tony's a good man. Firecracker suckered him into grabbing me. He thought it was a joke. Anyway, thanks for going along with my story."

"It was quite a story. You certainly do have an imagination. By the way, how's your ankle?" Karlee asked.

Rebecca grinned. "It's just fine. Thanks for asking."

"I can't believe that they bought that story. Even Mike, who usually questions everything, believed it. You're walking out of a store, turn your ankle, and some stranger comes to your rescue. And, he just turns out to be the brother of the worst person living in Cowtown. And, on top of that, it's love at first sight. How corny can you get?"

"Hey, like you said; they bought it. What can I say? Besides, how come you didn't tell me that you were dating a cop? Who just happens to be the cop who is investigating my kidnapping, by the way."

"And, also Mike getting shot," Karlee added.

"Mike seems to be doing okay, doesn't he?"

"Seems like it."

Rebecca smiled at her sister. "I'm sorry I didn't tell you the truth about Tony."

"It's okay. I'm sorry I didn't tell you about John," Karlee replied.

"One more thing. I'm just curious, so don't take this the wrong way."

"What's that?" Karlee asked.

"Was it you who tried to burn down Firecracker's house?"

Karlee looked surprised. "My God, Rebecca, why would you think that?"

"Well, it wasn't me. Mike was still in the hospital. Who does that leave?"

"A million other people who would like to see him dead, that's who," Karlee stated, emphatically.

"I'm glad it wasn't you. So, do you think this thing with the detective is going anywhere, or is it just a fling?"

Karlee smiled, her face lighting up at the mention of John. "I really like him, Rebecca. A lot."

Rebecca hugged her. "Good for you. Just promise me something."

"What's that?"

"Please don't tell him that Tony kidnapped me. I'd hate to see my future husband put in jail by your boyfriend."

Karlee laughed. "I promise. I've got to get going. I'm glad we talked. I hate it when we're mad at each other."

     "Me, too. Love ya."

     "Back atcha, sister."

Chapter Twenty-four

"Did you ever feel like there wasn't anyone in the world who didn't want you dead?" Freddie asked.

"Nope!"

"Well, that's how I feel," Freddie took another big swallow of beer, emptying his glass. He pushed his glass towards Pistol. "One more."

"How come you're so depressed?" Pistol asked as he set another beer in front of Freddie.

"You'd be depressed, too, if someone was trying to kill you."

"I guess."

"Did you know someone tried to burn my house down? With me in it, for god's sake."

"I heard."

"It's been a hard year, Pistol. First, that thing with my tires happened. That was downright mean, embarrassing me like that."

"I guess. But it was kinda funny."

"You think it was funny? I went to jail for six months because of that. Nothing funny about that," Freddie replied.

"You gotta learn to control that temper of yours. That's all."

"Nothing funny about me being shot in the back, either. Or, do you think that was funny, too?" Freddie said, starting to get upset.

"Nah. That was wack, man."

"Damn right it was," Freddie agreed. "I coulda been killed."

"You were lucky that night," Pistol said.

"Ya, I was."

"You were lucky you were awake when that fire started, too."

"I think I know who might have done that," Freddie told Pistol.

"Seriously? Did you tell the cops?"

"Hell, no, I didn't tell the cops. Anyway, I'm not one hundred percent sure."

"Who do you think it was?" Pistol asked.

"Forget it. Give me another beer."

"You better slow down, Freddie. It's early and, at the rate you're downing those beers, I'll be calling you a cab before long."

"What the fuck! Do ya think you're my mother? Just give me another beer, will ya?"

Across the room, sitting alone in a booth, a man watched as Freddie and Pistol conversed. He took a sip of his beer, put the glass down on the table, and took out his cell phone.

"He's here."

He listened to the voice on the other end and grinned. "No problem. At the rate he's drinking, he'll be out of it in no time. I'll call you in a little while with an update."

He ended the call and took another sip of beer.

"You're cut off. No more for you," Pistol told Freddie an hour later.

"That's bullshit, man. I'm fine to drive."

"No, you're not. Give me your keys."

"No fucking way you're getting my keys."

Pistol locked eyes with Freddie. "Yes, I am. You either hand them over right now or I'll take them from you."

Freddie was drunk but he still knew he should keep his mouth shut and hand Pistol the keys to his truck. He'd seen Pistol hurt more than one patron of the Squirrel House when they got smart with him. He reached into his pocket, pulled out his keys, and held them up so Pistol could see them.

"Are these want you want?" Freddie slurred.

As Pistol reached for the keys, Freddie pulled his hand back. Freddie laughed and held the keys out to Pistol again. Pistol reached for them the second time, and Freddie pulled the keys out of Pistol's reach.

Pistol's fist shot out and caught Freddie right on his nose, knocking him off the barstool and onto the floor.

"What the fuck, Pistol! Whatcha do that for?" Freddie cried out. "I'm bleeding."

Pistol walked around the bar, reached for Freddie's hand, and pulled him up off the floor.

"Keys. Now!"

Freddie handed him the keys. "I was gonna give them to you. You didn't have to punch me."

"Sometimes, you really get on my nerves, Freddie. Now go sit down in that empty booth over there. And, stay there. I'm calling you a cab."

"Come on, Pistol. I don't need a ride. Besides, I'm not ready to go home yet. How about one more beer?"

Pistol grabbed Freddie by the front of his shirt and pulled him close. "Go sit your ass down, Freddie," he said, quietly. "Don't make me tell you again."

Freddie took a step back, then practically fell as Pistol let go of his shirt, throwing him off balance.

"Alright. Geez. What's biting your ass, anyway?

Your old lady not giving you any?"

Pistol didn't think twice. He landed a solid punch to Freddie's jaw. Freddie was out before he hit the floor.

Pistol looked at Freddie lying on the floor and grinned. "Damn, that felt good," he uttered. He went back behind the bar and called for an Uber driver to come and take Freddie home.

The man, sitting in the booth, watched Freddie go down. He picked up his cell phone, punched in a number, and waited for an answer.

"It's me. Your friend isn't driving anywhere tonight. He's drunk and the bartender just knocked him flat on his ass."

He listened for a few seconds and laughed. "Ya, it was a pretty good hit. He's still on the floor. I know. I'm on it. Don't worry. I'll get it off before someone tries to start his car. Of course, I'll keep it. I'm not about to throw a bomb in the garbage."

He listened for a few more seconds and then ended the call.

She sat back and sighed. Oh, well, the best-laid plans of mice and men, often go. . . what? Is it astray or awry, she wondered, making a mental note to check it out.

Chapter Twenty-five

Freddie opened his front door and squinted, the sunlight hurting his eyes. "Detective."

"Freddie." Detective Peppers responded. "You look like hell. Rough night?"

"You might say that. What do you want now?" Freddie inquired.

"May I come in?" Detective Peppers asked.

"Is it necessary?"

"I'd like to talk to you."

Freddie grabbed the door to steady himself and grinned. "I guess I'm still a little drunk from last night."

"You better go sit down before you fall down," Peppers told him.

Freddie stepped aside to allow Peppers to enter, and quickly closed the front door. "Coffee?" he asked Peppers.

"Sounds good. Black, please."

"Ma," he yelled. "One more coffee. Black."

"Your mother is here?" Peppers said, stating the obvious.

"She comes over to clean. I'd like to hire a cleaning lady but mom insists she can do it better. What the hell? Why not if it makes her happy? Plus, it doesn't cost me anything, except for a dinner now and then."

Detective Peppers took the cup of coffee that Mrs. Demonti handed to him. "Thank you, ma'am."

"You're welcome. Freddie, is there anything else you need?"

"I'm good, Mom. Thanks."

"Well, I'll be off then. Enjoy your day, Detective."

"Thank you."

"Freddie, I'll talk to you about this later."

"Bye, Mom." Freddie waited until his mother left before he said, "I love that woman. I just wish I could get her to clean in the afternoon. But, nooo. She says I waste the day lying in bed until noon. I think she comes early just to bug me. Oh, well." Freddie looked over at Peppers. "What are you here for, anyway?"

"I've got some news I thought you'd be interested in hearing."

Freddie yawned. "Sorry. I need sleep. What would that be?"

"We know who shot you."

Freddie sat up straight and stared at Peppers. "You got the guy?"

"We do. He's in custody as we speak. I figured I'd tell you before you saw it on the news."

"So, who's the son of a bitch that shot me?"

"Manny Fitzgerald," Detective Peppers said, waiting to see what Freddie's reaction would be.

Freddie's mouth dropped open in surprise. "No fucking way."

"I couldn't believe it either. All these years we thought he was dead and, there he was, alive and enjoying life on an island in the Pacific."

"So, why'd he come back? It can't be because he wanted to shoot me. I never did nothing to him."

Suddenly, Freddie stood up. "Wait a minute. He killed his father, didn't he? My god, he shot his father right in front of his mother. What the hell, Detective? None of this makes sense."

"It does when you know the whole story."

"I'm not going anywhere. How about another cup of coffee?"

Detective Peppers waited until Freddie poured them each a second cup of coffee, then sat back, put his feet up on the coffee table, and looked at Freddie. "It gets a little confusing but I think you'll get the picture."

"Go on," Freddie prompted. "And, please take your shoes off my table."

"Sorry. I wasn't thinking." Peppers removed his feet from Freddie's coffee table. "As everyone knows, before Artie Fitzgerald retired, he was a big deal with the Chicago Outfit," Peppers said. "He started as a runner but he was smart. When he heard that the boss was looking for someone to take out a rival gang member, he volunteered. He made his bones when he was just seventeen, and from that point on he continued to move up the ladder. He became an enforcer, and he was good at it. He liked to hurt people and there are rumors that he beat a few men to death. He finally ended up an underboss. Pretty much stayed there until he got out of the business."

"I heard he never did any jail time," Freddie said.

"That's true. He was never convicted of anything. Arrested a few times but the witnesses either changed their testimony or disappeared."

"So, what does this have to do with me?"

"Hold on. Anyway, Artie got married and had two sons. Sammy and Manny. Martha, Artie's wife, tried to raise those two boys right but by the time they were out of high school, Artie had both of them working for him. Martha tried to put a stop to it but Artie wouldn't stand for her interfering with him and the boys. She wound up in the hospital on more than one occasion."

"He beat her?"

"Sure as hell did. The police always tried to get

her to file a complaint but she never would. Nothing they could do about it."

"Hitting a woman is the worst thing a man can do," Freddie commented.

"I agree."

"Go on," Freddie prompted.

"So, one day - it was late August and it was hot. Anyway, the two boys were out on a collection and the guy couldn't pay up. Sammy tells Manny to go get the bat out of the car. Manny walks out of the guy's store, and as he opens the trunk of the car, he hears a shot. He runs back into the store and sees that his brother is down. Figuring he's next, he hightails it out of there, jumps in his car, and takes off, leaving his brother bleeding to death on the dirty floor of the store. Manny goes home and tells his father what happened. His father, outraged because Manny didn't kill the guy that shot Sammy, proceeds to beat the crap out of him. He probably would have killed the kid, except Martha, who is witnessing all this, hits Artie over the head with a frying pan and knocks him out. Manny takes off and no one hears from him again. A few weeks later, his car is found abandoned on the side of the road, and everyone figures he's dead."

"Then, nine years later, he shows up and shoots his father," Freddie states.

"Right. Martha never got over losing her two sons that way. One gunned down in cold blood and the other one hiding from his father. She started drinking and when she drank, she mouthed off. When Artie got tired of hearing her crap, he'd hit her. They weren't the fierce beatings she used to get but he still slapped her around now and then. What Artie didn't know, is that Martha knew exactly where Manny was and every so often they talked to each other. During one of their conversations, Martha mentioned that Artie was still beating on her."

"So, Manny came back because he wanted to help his mother," Freddie stated.

"Exactly. His mother wouldn't leave his father or have him arrested. She was afraid of what Artie would do to her if she tried. So, Manny came back to the States – to Chicago – and waited for the right opportunity to kill his dad."

"Couldn't he find a better place than a restaurant, where there were dozens of witnesses?"

"At that point, I don't think he cared."

"What about Mikc Campanale? Why'd he shoot him?" Freddie asked.

"He got in the way. Collateral damage."

"And, me? What the hell did I ever do to him?"

Peppers grinned. "You're gonna love this. Do you remember Lori Simpson?"

Freddie looked confused. "Sure. What about her?"

"You remember asking her to the prom when you were a senior in high school?"

"Of course, I do. Man, I haven't thought about her for years. I really liked her." Freddie frowned. "I don't get it. What does my going to the prom with Lori have to do with anything?"

"Manny was supposed to take her to that prom. He was nuts over her. He had asked her and she had said yes. Then, you asked her and she broke off her date with Manny, so she could go with you. He never got over it."

"What the fuck, Peppers. Are you telling me that Manny shot me because Lori went to the prom with me and not him? That's crazy, man. That makes no sense."

"Manny isn't quite right in the head, so don't even try to make sense out of it. I guess when he saw you going into that tavern, it triggered something. He pulled out his gun and he shot you. It wasn't premeditated. You were just in the wrong place at the wrong time."

Freddie sat back and shook his head. "He told you all this shit? He confessed to everything?"

"He sang like a bird until his lawyer walked in. He'll go away but it will probably be a mental facility. He's not all there."

"What about torching my house? Did he do that, too?"

"I don't think so. I asked him about it but he denied knowing anything about it."

"Have you told Mike Campanale about this?"

"I'm going over there as soon I as leave. I think the whole Campanale family will be glad to find out that Mike wasn't the target."

"That's quite a story, Peppers. How'd you catch Manny, anyhow?"

"His mother called us. She turned him in. Then, as soon as we picked him up, she called an attorney for him."

"Are you shitting me? He kills his father to protect his mother and she turns him into the police? This whole fucking world has gone nuts."

"Manny was staying with her, hiding in her house. It didn't take much for her to realize that he was a little off and needed some help. She probably wouldn't have called us if he had just killed Artie. She was glad to see the old bastard gone. But, Manny started talking and he told her about shooting you, just to get even for something that happened way back in high school. She figured maybe he had stayed in the hot sun too long and it had fried his brain. Anyway, it makes no difference now. She called us and we went over and picked him up. No fuss, at all. He actually seemed glad to see us."

"Well, that's a couple of unsolved crimes you can close the book on," Freddie commented.

"Actually, three," said Peppers. "You, Mike and old man Fitzgerald, and what happened to Manny all those years ago. Here we all thought he was dead and all this time he was living on a tropical island."

"Three it is," Freddie agreed.

"I guess that's it," Peppers said, as he stood up. "I'll let you know if I find out anything else about your house being set on fire."

"Thanks," said Freddie, not getting up.

"Don't get up," Peppers remarked, "I'll let myself out. By the way, what happened to your nose?"

Freddie grinned. "It ran into a fist. Hurts like hell."

Peppers laughed. "Ya. It looks pretty sore. Your fault?"

"Isn't it always," Freddie replied.

Chapter Twenty-six

"So, what's the big news?" Karlee asked Mike, as she grabbed a can of pop out of his refrigerator. "You sounded pretty excited when you called."

"Your boyfriend is on his way over."

"John?"

"Ya. He said he had news about the shooting."

"Your shooting?"

"That's what he said. He said he wanted to tell the whole family all at once," Mike answered.

"Did you call Rebecca, too?" Karlee inquired.

"I left a voice mail. God only knows where she's at or what she's up to."

"Are Mom and Dad coming over?"

"I don't think so. I didn't call them and Peppers didn't mention them. He just said to call you and Rebecca."

"I guess he'll talk to them after he sees us."

"I guess," Mike said.

Karlee turned, as Emmy Lou walked into the kitchen, dressed in her pajamas. She yawned. "Sorry. I had a late night."

"Are you just getting up?" Karlee asked her. "It's almost noon."

"I said, I had a late night. What's happening?"

"Detective Peppers is on his way over," Mike replied. "It seems he has some news about the shooting."

"About your shooting?" Emmy Lou asked.

"It looks like Rebecca just pulled up in front," Karlee said, as she looked out the window.

"And, it looks like your boyfriend is pulling in

right behind her."

"Did you make any coffee?" Emmy Lou asked Mike.

"I did, my love. Four hours ago, while you were snoring your pretty little head off."

"I don't snore," Emmy Lou said, defensively.

"Oh, yes, you definitely snore," Mike said. "Karlee, does our little Emmy Lou snore?"

Karlee grinned. "Like a lumberjack. Only louder."

There was a light knock on the front door, it opened, and Rebecca walked in with Detective Peppers right on her heels.

"Morning," said Emmy Lou.

Rebecca looked at her, wondering why she was still in her pajamas. "Do you realize it's after twelve o'clock?"

"Hi, Karlee," Peppers said.

"Hi. What's the big news?"

"First, I want to thank you all for getting together. It's so much easier than talking to each of you separately. We could have done this at the station but I thought you'd all be more comfortable here."

"No problem," said Mike.

"We know who shot you, Mike," Peppers said. "He's been arrested."

"Oh, Mike, did you hear that? They got the guy," Emmy Lou exclaimed.

"I heard him..."

"It was Firecracker, wasn't it?" Emmy Lou said, interrupting Mike before he could finish. "I knew it. I hope you lock him up forever and that no good bastard rots in jail," she exclaimed.

Everyone stared at Emmy Lou for a few seconds,

wondering about her outburst. Finally, Mike said, "How about we all get comfortable in the living room? Detective, can I get you something to drink?"

"A cold drink would be nice," Peppers answered.

"Coke or Pepsi?"

"Coke's fine," replied Peppers.

"Coming right up," Mike said. He opened the refrigerator and took out a can of Coke. "So, who shot me?" Mike asked as he handed Peppers the can.

"Well, I'm sorry if this disappoints you, Emmy Lou, but it wasn't Freddie Demonti who shot Mike. It was Manny Fitzgerald."

He waited, knowing first there would be a few seconds of silence, and then the questions would start flying.

"Now, perhaps, you all would like to apologize to me," Rebecca said, a smug look on her face.

"What in the world for?" Mike asked.

"I told you I saw him in the restaurant that night. You all treated me like I was crazy. So, I expect all of you to tell me that you're sorry."

Everyone stared at Rebecca.

"Karlee, would you like to start?" Rebecca asked, grinning.

"Screw you, Rebecca. I'm not apologizing to you for anything."

"How about you, Mike? Emmy Lou?"

"Sorry, Rebecca," Emmy Lou replied.

"Mike?" Rebecca asked. "Anything you want to say?"

"Ya. I'm sorry I have a crazy-ass sister. Detective, please, go on. You must have quite a story to tell."

"I do," said Peppers. "And, I'd like you all to do me

a favor if you would. Please, call me John."

Peppers sat back in the chair, took a swallow of his pop, and started talking.

Fifteen minutes later, Emmy Lou asked, "How can you be sure he shot Mike?"

"Once again, Emmy Lou, Manny confessed that he did it. Mike was not his target. Manny's father was. Shooting Mike was an accident," Peppers said.

"Maybe he's lying. I don't believe it. I think it was Firecracker. Or, maybe Firecracker hired Manny to shoot all of us."

"Why would he do that?" Rebecca asked Emmy Lou.

"Maybe he was trying to get even for something that some people might have done."

"Emmy Lou, I hate to say this but you're talking a little crazy," said Karlee. "If John says that it was Manny that did the shooting, then it was Manny. Don't forget that he tried to kill Firecracker, too."

"They probably set it up so that Firecracker would look innocent," Emmy said.

Karlee looked at her brother. "Mike, is Emmy Lou okay?"

"If you have a question about me, ask me," Emmy Lou shouted. "I'm right here in the room. And, no. I'm not okay. I'm tired, and I don't feel good. Screw this. I'm going back to bed."

"Sorry. Emmy Lou hasn't been herself lately," Mike remarked, as Emmy Lou stormed out of the room.

"Don't worry about it," Peppers said. "Everyone has an off day now and then."

"I can hear you!" Emmy Lou yelled. "Stop talking

about me!"

Detective Peppers left a few minutes after Mike apologized for Emmy Lou's strange behavior.

"Do you have any idea what that was all about?" Rebecca asked Mike.

"All I know is that ever since Demonti's release from prison, Emmy Lou's been obsessed with him. She was positive he tried to kill all of us in the restaurant and that he won't quit until we are all dead. She thinks he's following her all the time. I can't figure it out. After finding out that it wasn't Firecracker who did the shooting, you would think she would be relieved. Instead, she's more upset than ever," Mike said.

"Well, Tony told me from the beginning that it wasn't Firecracker that shot Mike and that other guy," Rebecca stated.

"Artie Fitzgerald," said Karlee.

"What?" asked Rebecca.

"The other man's name is Artie Fitzgerald," Karlee replied.

"I know that. Why are you telling me that?"

"You said the other guy. I just thought I would remind you of his name," Karlee said.

Rebecca stared at her. "Whatever. Like I was saying before you interrupted me - Tony said that Firecracker swore to him that he didn't shoot anyone. He also said that his brother promised that he would never do anything to hurt any of us. Tony said he believed him. I believe Tony. I don't think we have anything to worry about."

Mike looked skeptical. "I don't know, Rebecca. You three are still probably on his shit list for that tire thing. He went to jail because of you guys."

"He went to jail because he beat up some guy in the park," Karlee interjected. "Not because of what we did."

"But one act led to the other," Mike responded.

"Well, I, for one, am going to take what Tony said at face value and put this all behind me. I hope you guys can do the same," said Rebecca. "As far as Emmy Lou is concerned - I don't know, Mike. If she doesn't snap out of it, you might consider getting her some help."

"What? Now, you think she's nuts or something?" Mike said, raising his voice.

"Who's nuts?"

Mike turned to see Emmy Lou standing in the doorway of the kitchen, listening to their conversation. "No one is nuts, baby. We were just saying that we hope this is the end of anything to do with Firecracker."

Emmy Lou looked at him and smiled. "I'm sorry I blew before. I guess I was surprised that it was someone else who shot you. I was so sure it was Firecracker."

"Are you feeling better?" Karlee asked her.

"A little. Do we have any ginger ale in the house, Mike?" Emmy Lou asked.

"Tummy ache, honey?" he asked.

"Kind of," she replied.

"Why don't you go lay down on the couch and I'll bring you something to drink," Mike told her.

"Ginger ale. If you don't have any, then a glass of water will do."

Rebecca stood and grabbed her purse off the kitchen counter. "Well, I'm off. See you guys."

"Wait. I'll walk out with you," said Karlee. "Bye,

Mike. Emmy Lou."

"Take care," Mike said, kissing his sisters goodbye.

"He's wrong, you know," Emmy Lou said emphatically, as soon as Mike shut the door.

Mike looked confused. "Who's wrong, sweetie?"

"That cop. He might believe that cock and bull story about Manny Fitzgerald shooting you by mistake but I sure don't. He's taking the fall for Firecracker."

Mike sat down on the couch next to her and took her hand. "I'm not sure if that's the case but it's a possibility," he said, not wanting to start an argument by disagreeing with her. "But what would Manny have to gain by trying to kill us? He doesn't even know us."

Emmy Lou sighed. "Am I the only one who sees what actually happened? Money, of course. Isn't everything about money?"

"You think Freddie hired Manny to shoot us? That might be but how did Freddie even know Manny was still alive? I mean, everyone believed Manny died nine years ago. So, how did Freddie know where he was?"

Emmy Lou stared at Mike, with a confused look on her face. "Well, I haven't figured it all out yet," she finally said. "My God, Mike, do I have to do everything?"

Chapter Twenty-seven

Freddie looked at his watch. Perfect. She should be on her way to work. He picked up his phone, hit sixty-six on the keypad, and waited. She didn't pick up, of course. She had stopped answering her phone over a week ago. Freddie left a brief message and ended the call.

He had called her at 7:45 a.m., every weekday for over two weeks now. The first few days she had talked to him and asked him not to call again. After that, when she found out that it was him calling, she hung up. Now, she didn't even answer the phone.

Freddie had left the same message now for the past five days. "I know it was you. We need to talk."

She wasn't exactly afraid of Freddie. She couldn't exactly put her finger on what she actually felt. At first, when he started calling, she would get a sinking feeling in her stomach when she realized it was him. Then, when she no longer answered his calls, she would just smile when her cell rang at 7:45. It was like they were playing some kind of a game.

She would wait a minute or so, and then play his message. She knew what it was going to be, as it was always the same nine words.

Today, as she drove to work, her thoughts wandered to Freddie Demonti, and the night she threw that bomb through his window. Well, it wasn't really a bomb. If I had a real bomb that night, she thought, he might be dead instead of bugging me with these messages.

The ringing of her cell phone brought her back to

reality. As usual, she didn't answer and waited for the ringtone, indicating that she had a voice message. She smiled when she heard the music. Right on time, aren't you, Freddie, she thought. She picked up her phone and listened to the message. Suddenly, she felt sick to her stomach.

She pulled over to the side of the road and stopped her car, not quite sure if she was going to throw up. She took a couple of deep breaths, decided she was okay, and laid her head back against the headrest.

After a few minutes, she listened to the message again, opened the car door, and threw up on the side of the road.

She looked up, as a car pulled in her behind her and stopped. A cop got out of his vehicle and walked toward her. "Ma'am, you can't park here. You'll need to move on," he said.

"I know, Officer. I'm going."

The cop looked down at the ground and realized he was standing in her vomit. "Are you okay, Ma'am? Do you need an ambulance?"

She gave him a weak smile. "No, I'm fine. It must have been something I ate for breakfast. Sorry."

"Are you sure you're okay to drive?"

"Really, I'm okay. I better get going or I'll be late for work. Thank you for stopping to check on me."

"Alright, then. Take care, Ma'am."

She took a deep breath, started her car, and carefully merged into the traffic.

She checked in the rearview mirror to be sure that the cop wasn't behind her, picked up her phone, and made a call. When he didn't answer, she left a message telling him to contact her immediately.

Chapter Twenty-eight

"Well, isn't this nice?" Cecelia Campanale said as she sat down at the dining room table. She smiled at everyone and then looked at Rebecca. "Rebecca, would you care to say grace?"

Karlee glanced over at Rebecca and grinned, wondering what was coming next.

Rebecca met her mother's eyes and smiled. "I'd love to, Mom," she replied.

Mike and her father looked surprised. Rebecca looked at her father, who was sitting at the head of the table, and said, "Let us all bow our heads." She waited until everyone had complied and said, "Dear Lord, thank you for this food that you have provided and for our mother who has prepared it for us. Thank you for healing Mike and for bringing him and Emmy Lou together. We welcome John here today and ask that you watch over him as he watches over our city and keeps us safe. Thank you for my mother and father, who have taught Mike, Karlee, and me your ways and continue to help us and guide us. We love them for all they do for us. Thank you for bringing Tony into my life. He is my shining light and my bright future. Please watch over him and keep him safe. Thank you for my sister, who is also my best friend. If it wasn't for her, I wouldn't be the person I am today."

Rebecca stopped talking and cleared her throat. She looked over at Karlee. Karlee opened her eyes and mouthed, "What are you doing?"

Rebecca grinned. "Sorry. I had a little frog in my throat," she said. She continued her prayer. "Also, God, please take care of Buttercup. I know he's getting old and will soon be in doggy heaven but if and when you feel the need to take him, please let him go peacefully into your loving arms. Please continue to watch over all our grandmas, grandpas, aunts, uncles, and cousins, which are still living here in this sinful world, and keep them safe. Bless our President who needs all the help you can give him. Please continue to take care of Mrs. Monthie, my parents' neighbor, who hasn't been feeling too well lately. Also, if it isn't too much to ask, my car..."

"Rebecca?" her father interrupted. "I think you've covered everything. The food's getting cold. Are you about done?"

Rebecca looked at her father, pretending to be surprised at the interruption. "I'm sorry, Dad. It's just that I didn't want to miss anyone. I'll finish up."

"We'd all appreciate that," her father replied, trying to stay serious.

Rebecca looked at Karlee and grinned. Karlee lost it, and the two sisters started laughing out loud. Mike, who was trying his best to hold his composure, let loose and snorted. That was all it took for everyone at the table to start laughing. Except for Mrs. Campanale, who just sat there, disgusted by the way everyone was acting. She picked up her spoon and started clinking it on her wine glass.

"That's enough now. Will everyone please settle down? I don't appreciate everyone laughing while we're praising God." Angry over being ignored, she hit the glass harder, breaking it and spilling red wine all over her white tablecloth.

She looked at the mess, pushed her chair back, stood up, and yelled, "Will everyone please shut the fuck up?"

The room went dead quiet.

"Thank you," Cecelia said. "Rebecca, please finish your prayer before this meal is a total disaster. Karlee, just a head's up. You're saying grace next time."

Rebecca laughed.

"Rebecca!" her mom yelled.

"Sorry, Mom," she said.

Trying not to laugh out loud again, Rebecca said, "I'll finish up."

"Please do," her mother told her.

She closed her eyes and bowed her head. "I guess that's it, God. Mom's hungry and when she gets hungry, she can get mean. So, here goes. Thanks for the food, thanks for the wine, thanks for good health, okay, let's dine."

Cecelia stared at her, shook her head in disgust, and sat down. "I'm sorry you gentlemen had to see that disgusting display by my daughter," she said to Tony and John. "I thought we raised her properly but, obviously, something went wrong. Tony, you might want to rethink your decision about marrying her."

Tony smiled. "I think you did a wonderful job, Mrs. Campanale. I think it is obvious, however, that she still needs some work. I'm always up for a challenge and I'll do my best to turn her into the best daughter you could ask for."

"Please, call me Cecelia. Well, if you still want her, after that little show she just put on, you have my blessing."

Tony fixed eyes with Rebecca, who was staring at him. "Oh, I want her, all right. And, don't you worry, Cecelia. I'll fix her real good."

Rebecca stuck out her tongue at him. "I don't

need no fixing," she said, smiling. "I good just the way I is. Don't you know?"

"Would someone please pass me the potatoes," Mr. Campanale asked. "I'm starving."

An hour later everyone was still at the table, enjoying a cup of coffee and conversing. Now that everyone was done eating and her cooking had received the proper accolades, Mrs. Campanale had settled down and was finally enjoying herself.

"Tell me, John," Mr. Campanale said, "do you have any idea who it was that kidnapped Rebecca?"

Rebecca looked questioningly at Karlee. Karlee gave her a reassuring smile. Rebecca smiled back, waiting to hear John's reply.

"You know, Victor, that's one of the weirdest cases we've ever had. Your daughter was grabbed right in front of her apartment building, held in a basement for five days, and then freed. No one saw anything and we haven't got a clue. We still haven't figured out the reason she was taken. She wasn't harmed in any way and there was no request for ransom money. So, the answer to your question is no. We don't know who it was."

"Well, at least my little girl is safe and sound," Victor commented.

John glanced over at Rebecca. "Yes, she certainly is. Aren't you, Rebecca?"

Rebecca looked over at him. "I'm sorry, John. Did you ask me something? I was thinking about something else."

John held her gaze for a couple of seconds. "Not important," he said and looked away.

"What about Freddie Demonti? Do you know who tried to fry that son of a bitch?" Mike asked John.

"Mike!" Karlee said.

"Oh, my god," Mike said. "Tony, I am so sorry. I wasn't thinking."

"Don't worry about it," Tony told him. "Sometimes even I forget that we're brothers. Actually, we're half-brothers. I know he isn't well-liked in Cowtown but I think someone trying to burn him alive was a pretty rotten thing to do."

"You're right, Tony," John replied. "Unfortunately, we haven't got a clue as to who did it."

"I hope you won't give up on it," Tony said.

"We won't. I don't have much hope that we'll ever find the guy that did it, though."

"Are you sure it was a guy?" Karlee inquired.

John looked surprised at her question. "Do you think a woman did it?" he asked Karlee.

Everyone's eyes were on Karlee, waiting for her answer. She shrugged. "How would I know? I just meant, how can you be sure it was a man, that's all?"

"Could we please change the subject?" Cecelia asked. "I'm sick and tired of hearing about that man."

"I agree," said Victor. He looked over at Tony and asked, "Just what exactly is it you do, Tony?"

"Well, I still think he shot Mike and wants to kill all of us," Emmy Lou exclaimed before Tony could answer Victor's question.

Mike took a deep breath and blew it out. "Please, Emmy Lou. Let's not go there. Firecracker did not try to kill us, nor did he hire Manny Fitzgerald to kill us. Case closed!"

Emmy Lou gave him a dirty look. "You may have

closed the case, Mike, but I haven't."

"John, tell her," Mike implored.

"I have, Mike. You know that. I can only give her the facts. I can't make her believe them."

"Emmy Lou, you need to stop this nonsense!" Cecelia yelled.

"Whoa, Mom. Where did that come from?" Mike said, surprised at his mother's outburst.

"I'm sorry for yelling at you, Emmy Lou. But we all need to forget about Freddie Demonti and get on with our lives."

Emmy Lou stared at her, shocked at being yelled at. Her bottom lip started to quiver, and tears started rolling down her cheeks. She pushed back her chair and stood up.

"I want to go home," she mumbled through her tears. "Are you coming, Mike? Or, do I have to walk?"

"Emmy Lou, please. You're being silly?" Mike said.

Emmy Lou glared at him, turned around, and walked out of the house.

Karlee kicked Mike under the table.

"What the hell, Karlee? What did you do that for?"

"Get your ass out of that chair and go after her, you idiot," Karlee told him.

Mike looked at his father. "Dad?"

"Do what she says, Mike. You'll never win a fight with a woman, so don't even try. Just go apologize."

"But I didn't do anything wrong," Mike said.

"It doesn't make any difference if you did or didn't. You better go after her."

Mike got up from the table, shaking his head in total confusion. He looked over at Tony and John, who were grinning. "What's so damned funny?" he said.

"Nothing," Tony replied, still smiling.

"I hope you remember this when you're in my shoes, and running after the woman you love like a puppy dog. Then, I'll be the one laughing."

"Not me," said Tony. "You won't ever see me chasing after Rebecca."

"Really?" remarked Rebecca.

"Really," Tony replied.

Mike looked at the two of them and decided to get out of there and find Emmy Lou. He didn't want to be around when Rebecca lost it, which was about to happen. He'd been on the other end of that temper, and it wasn't pretty.

Chapter Twenty-nine

"Shouldn't you be at work?" Karlee asked.

"I got off early, so I could talk to you. I want you to hear a voice message I got from Freddie Demonti last week."

Karlee watched as the woman took out her cell phone and started playing the recording.

As Karlee listened to the voice mail message, she looked more and more shocked, "My God!" she exclaimed when the message ended. "That's horrible. You've got to call the police."

"No. I'm not talking to the police."

"Will you let John listen to it? Maybe it could be off the record. You know, like talking to a friend. At least, he could give you some advice on what to do."

"No! He's a cop and would want to pursue this. You know that, as well as I do. You promised me you wouldn't say anything, Karlee. I'm holding you to that promise."

"That was before you got this message. How'd he get your phone number, anyway?"

"I have no idea but you can't say anything about this."

Karlee frowned. "This isn't the first message he's left you, is it?"

"The other ones weren't like this. They just said that he knew what I did and that we needed to talk."

"How many other ones were there? Two? Three?"

"More, I guess."

"How many? Ten?"

The woman did not answer her.

"More than that?" Karlee persisted.

"He's called every day for the past couple of weeks. It's always at the same time but never on weekends."

"Well, this has to stop right now. I'm calling John and telling him that Firecracker is harassing you," Karlee said.

"Don't you dare! If you break your promise, I'll never trust you again. I only wanted you to hear this in case something happens to me."

"This is bullshit. You know that?"

"Karlee, I'll handle it. Please, don't say anything."

"Play the message one more time," Karlee said.

"What in the world for? It's gross."

"I know it's gross. Just play it, will you?"

The woman hit the play button on her phone and waited for Freddie Demonti to start talking.

"Time's up, bitch. You should have answered your phone and talked to me. You need to be punished for what you did. Are you paying attention, bitch? Because here's what's going to happen. When you least expect it, you're gonna be - Whoa. I almost ruined the surprise. But I will tell you that it involves cocks. Lots of them. All for you, bitch. I bet you're getting wet..."

"I can't listen to any more of this crap. It's making me sick. Turn it off," Karlee exclaimed.

"You wanted to hear it, so don't yell at me. I'm erasing it."

"No!" Karlee cried out. "We need it for evidence, in case something happens to you."

"Sorry, Karlee."

"Did you just erase it?"

"I did."

"Do you know how dumb that was?" Karlee asked.

"Don't call me dumb. I shouldn't have told you about this in the first place. It was a mistake. Just forget it."

Karlee stared at her. "Forget it? Firecracker just threatened to have you gang-raped, and you want me to forget it?"

"Please. I'll handle it?"

"How? Just how do you think you are going to handle it?"

"I have a plan."

Karlee shook her head in disgust. "You have a plan. Isn't that wonderful? Why couldn't you have just let everything go? What could you have been thinking when you threw that bomb into his house?"

"I wanted to kill him for hurting Mike. Firecracker's no good, Karlee. You know that. I wanted to get rid of him once and for all."

"But we all know he didn't shoot Mike."

"Maybe he didn't shoot him. But what about that horrible beating he gave him? He hurt Mike really bad. I'm sorry, Karlee, if you don't approve of what I did but that son of a bitch needs to die."

"You have to drop this shit. Now!"

"A little too late, don't you think? What I have to do is watch my back and be sure I get him before he gets me."

"You're acting crazy, you know that? I'm telling John and Mike what's going on," said Karlee.

"The hell you are. You mention one word of this to anyone and you'll be sorry."

"I'll be sorrier if something happens to you."

"I'm tougher than you know, Karlee. Nothing is going to happen. I promise."

Karlee sighed. "Alright. I won't say anything. For now! But, if anything..."

"I've got to get going. Please, don't worry. I'll call you later."

She picked up her purse and walked to the front door. She turned and smiled at Karlee. "I love you, you know."

Karlee smiled back at her. "I know. I love you, too."

Karlee closed her front door, and leaned back, resting her body against it. Her head was spinning with what she had just heard. Firecracker had made a serious threat, and there was no doubt in her mind that he would follow through on it. After all, he had Rebecca kidnapped. But he didn't do anything after that, she thought. Maybe, he's all talk and no action. Nevertheless, if that message was meant to scare the hell out of someone, he had certainly succeeded.

Karlee had made a promise but she knew that she wouldn't be able to keep it. She wasn't sure if that crazy-ass Firecracker would follow through on his threat and the risk was too great to stay quiet.

She picked up her phone and called John. She listened while his phone rang. Then, she ended the call before he had a chance to answer. Damn, she thought. I can't do this. What if Firecracker is just blowing hot air, and doesn't do anything? If I tell John what she did, she could go to jail and it would be my fault.

Karlee jumped as her phone rang, scaring her.

"Hello."

"Hi. Did you just call?"

"Sorry about that. I hit the wrong speed dial

number."

"You have me on your speed dial?" John asked. "I'm flattered."

Karlee laughed. "You're my number two," she said.

"Just two? Who's number one?"

"911. You know, in case I need a cop," Karlee replied.

"I'm a cop. I respond to emergencies all the time."

"I do believe I might have an emergency after all. I think I need someone to come over and put out my fire."

John laughed. "I'll be there in ten minutes."

Chapter Thirty

Freddie wasn't in the least bit concerned that there would be hell to pay for the calls he had made. If she contacted the police, she would have to admit that it was her that tried to burn down his house. He was positive that wasn't going to happen.

He quit calling her after he left the message where he threatened her. He decided it might be a good idea to keep his mouth shut for a while. There were plenty of other ways to intimidate her.

He had started following her, making sure she knew he was on her tail. There was no way she could miss his truck but to be sure she knew he was there, he would pass her on the tollway and then slow down to let her get ahead of him. A few times, as he passed her car, he had even waved to her. The last time he waved, she gave him the finger, making him laugh. The woman has moxie, he thought.

With each day, the desire for revenge lessened, and by Friday night Freddie had decided to let the whole thing drop. He figured he had turned her into a nervous wreck.

So, by the end of the week, Freddie was pretty much over it and was sitting in the Squirrel House Tavern, talking to Frank, the owner of the bar.

"Busy tonight," Freddie commented, referring to a packed bar.

"Friday nights usually are busy," Frank said.

"This week flew by."

"They all fly by. I don't know where the hell the time goes. Before long it will be Christmas," Frank said.

"What the fuck, Frank. You're kinda pushing it,

don't you think? We haven't even celebrated the fourth of July yet. It's a long way to Christmas."

"Ya. Just a blink of the eye away."

"I guess," Freddie mumbled.

"Are you planning on staying sober tonight?" Frank asked.

"Don't worry. I'm not gonna start anything. I'm leaving in a little while. I've got a date."

Frank looked surprised. "A real date?" he asked.

"What? Do you think I can't get a real woman to go out with me? I'm a hell of a catch."

Frank laughed. "You are that. You're rich and good-looking. You have a big beautiful house and some really expensive cars. You've got a build that most men would give their right arm for. Plus, you have the biggest dick in town. That all sounds good, except you are the biggest dick in town. No woman will ever put up with that temper of yours."

"I can change."

"Freddie, you'll never change. So, has your date got a name?"

"You don't know her."

"I bet I do. I bet it's Rosy Palm and her five sisters."

"Funny, Frank. Real funny."

"Come on. Don't get pissed. I was just fooling with you."

Frank looked over at Pistol, who was tending bar. "Pistol, give Freddie another beer. On the house."

"Thanks," Freddie said. "That's my last one. I gotta get going."

Frank saw a man, at the other end of the bar, wave to him. "Excuse me, Freddie, I need to talk to that guy."

"I know him," Freddie said. "That's Pete Crasley. He owes me money."

Frank hesitated, wondering what Freddie was going to do. "You can catch him later. Right now, I need to talk to him. Okay?"

"No problem. I know where he lives."

"See ya, Freddie," Frank said and walked down to the other end of the bar.

Freddie picked up his glass and took a long swallow. He scanned the room, checking to see if there was anyone else there that he knew. He studied a man sitting alone in a booth, looking at his phone. Freddie thought he looked familiar but couldn't remember where he knew him from. Losing interest in him, Freddie continued to check out the rest of the patrons, surprised that there wasn't anyone there that he knew.

He downed the rest of his beer, got off his barstool, and walked towards the door. "See you later," he said to Pistol. As he walked past Frank, who was having an animated conversation with Pete Crasley, he gave him a wave.

At that exact moment, the man in the booth dialed a number, which activated a one-minute delay button on the bomb under Freddie's SUV.

Freddie reached into his pocket for his keys and swore when he realized that he had left them lying on the bar. As he turned around in the doorway and started to walk back into the bar, Pistol yelled 'catch' and threw Freddie his keys. Freddie reached out to catch them, missed, and swore again as the keys landed on the floor.

Frank, who had witnessed the scene, laughed.

"Nice catch," he said, sarcastically.

Freddie grinned at him and bent down to pick up his keys. "I never could catch worth a damn," he said.

"What the fuck was that?" yelled Pistol.

"That sounded like an explosion," exclaimed Frank.

"Nooo!" yelled Freddie, as he ran out the door towards his truck, and saw that his truck was on fire.

"Fire extinguisher! Someone bring me a fucking fire extinguisher. Now! Call the fire department! My truck's on fire," he screamed.

Pistol came running, carrying a fire extinguisher, and handed it to Freddie. Freddie took it from Pistol, started to open the truck door, and pulled his hand back.

"Damn, that's hot." He took the fire extinguisher and smashed it against the window. "Did you call the fire department?" he yelled at Pistol, as he hit the window again.

"Frank's on it," Pistol told him. "What are you doing?"

"What the hell does it look like? I'm trying to break this fucking window, so I can put the fire out."

"That window isn't gonna break. It's shatterproof."

Freddie looked at Pistol, realizing that he was right. There was no way he was going to be able to break that window.

Pistol stood on the sidewalk, watching Freddie. "Man, that stinks," he commented. "It's a good thing you weren't in there when that bomb went off. We'd be smelling you getting fried, instead of your leather seats."

Freddie looked away, not wanting Pistol to see the tears running down his face.

The man in the booth did not join the crowd that rushed outside to see the fire. He held his phone to his ear and waited for her to answer her phone.

"It didn't work," he said when she picked up.

"What do you mean, it didn't work? The bomb didn't go off?"

"Oh, it went off alright. But he wasn't in the truck at the time."

"What happened?"

"I set the timer, just like we planned. I figured he'd be in his car in less than a minute. It was parked right out front. Then, all of a sudden, the idiot walks back into the tavern."

"What?"

"He forgot his keys on the bar. How lucky can one person be?"

"How bad was the explosion? Would it have killed him?"

"I'm not sure. I haven't gone outside yet to look but I don't think it was as bad as I figured it would be. I guess next time I'll have to make sure I use more explosives."

"There won't be a next time."

"There won't?"

"No. I think we need to find a different way to get rid of him. Are you any good with a gun?"

"Fair."

"Maybe you should start going to the firing range and practice. Go take a look at his truck and call me back.

"Why?"

"I want to know how much damage there is, that's

why."

"Probably a lot."

"Well, go take a picture and send it to me."

"Maybe, you should just drop this. It's starting to get out of hand. If we get caught, we're both going to wind up in jail."

"As long as we're careful, we're not going to get caught. Just go take a picture, will you?"

"Alright, I will. God! Did I ever tell you that you're a huge pain in the ass?"

"Aren't all sisters?"

Chapter Thirty-one

"What the hell!" Freddie exclaimed as Detective Peppers walked toward him. "Are you the only cop in Chicago?"

Peppers laughed. "There are a few others. Why?"

"Well, you're the only one who shows up when there's trouble around here."

"I guess I always pull the short straw. So, what happened here, Freddie?"

"Someone put a bomb in my truck. Didn't you see that fucking mess sitting out front?"

"I did. It looks like someone really wants you dead. Was there a note this time, too?"

"Hell, no, I don't have a note. Besides, if there had been a note, don't you think it would have been destroyed by the fire?"

"So, there's no note," Peppers said.

"What the hell, Peppers? Are you on something? I just said that there was no note."

"Sorry. It's been a long day. Let's go sit in a booth."

Freddie picked up his glass of beer and walked over to an empty booth. "Is this one okay?"

"It'll do," Peppers replied. "So, Freddie, who's trying to kill you?" he asked, as soon as they were seated.

Freddie, obviously still upset from his ordeal, put his face in his hands, trying to hide his emotions.

"You need a hanky?" Peppers asked.

Freddie's head jerked up, and he stared at Peppers. "You being a smart ass, Peppers? Do you have any idea how much that truck cost? I love that truck and now it's ruined. It's gonna cost a fucking fortune to try to get it repaired. And, that's if it can even be repaired."

"I always wondered about that, Freddie. What does something like that cost? Three or four hundred?"

Freddie snorted. "I wish. That baby cost me almost six and that was a deal. The starting price is around six-thirty."

"The insurance on it must be out of this world," Peppers stated.

"You have no idea," Freddie said.

"I'm gonna take a look at Frank's security cameras and see if they show anything. If we're lucky, they'll be something on them that can help us."

"That bomb could have been planted any place and at any time," Freddie said, and gave a big sigh. "I'm so tired of having to watch my back, wondering what's gonna happen next."

"I imagine you are. It must be exhausting. Have you ever wondered if that's how those people who owe you money feel? You know - not knowing when you or one of your goons is gonna show up and break a leg or worse. It must be tough on them, too."

Freddie glared at him. "You don't know what the hell you're talking about."

"Sure I do," Peppers declared. "I'm gonna go talk to Frank. Let me know if you come up with anything."

Freddie watched as Peppers walked over and started talking to Frank. After a few minutes, the two men walked into Frank's office. Freddie took a deep breath and let it out, trying to compose himself.

Suddenly, he remembered that he had forgotten about his date. He picked up his beer glass and threw it against the wall, smashing it to pieces. Pistol started to reach for the baseball bat, then looked over at the booth, saw Freddie sitting there, and frowned.

"What the hell, Freddie?"

"Sorry. Put it on my tab."

"Damn right it's going on your tab." Pistol looked at Freddie and, for a brief moment, felt sorry for him. "Just take it easy, okay?" he yelled at Freddie.

Freddie took out his phone and called for a cab. He was tired. He was going home.

"I think Freddie got here around eight-thirty," Frank told Detective Peppers.

"Let's start around that time, then," Peppers said. "Let's hope that whoever planted that bomb did it while Freddie's truck was parked out front."

"You still believe in Santa Claus, too?" Frank asked, smiling.

"I know. It's asking a lot. Just hoping that all."

"Here we are. Time shows eight-fifteen. Let's start here."

"Can you speed it up just a little?" Peppers asked, after watching the monitor for a few minutes.

"Sure. Just watch closely. We don't want to miss anything."

The two men concentrated on the monitor, waiting to see Freddie's truck pull up in front of the tavern.

"There he is," Frank exclaimed.

"It's eight-forty," Peppers said, noting the time in the corner of the monitor. "What time did the bomb go off?"

Frank glanced up at a clock hanging on his office wall. "It's past ten, right now. Freddie wasn't here that long. He was just leaving when the bomb went off. He said he had a date. I'd say it was just a little after nine," he told Peppers.

"He had a date?" Peppers asked. "A real date?"

"He said it was. He was pretty hyped up about it."

"I'll be damned. I can't believe there's a woman out there who wants to date him," Peppers said, grinning.

"Well, miracles have been known to happen."

"Who's that?" Peppers suddenly exclaimed and pointed to a figure standing next to Freddie's truck. "Stop it and go back. Can you freeze it?"

Frank backed up the video and hit the pause button. Peppers stared at the figure on the monitor. "Can you make him out?" he asked Frank.

"I'm not sure. Maybe if I slow it down, we can get a better view."

Frank and Peppers watched as the figure, still standing next to Freddie's truck, dropped something on the sidewalk.

"What was that?" Frank said. "He dropped something."

"I think he dropped his keys. Can you zoom in on it?"

"Is this better?" Frank asked.

"Much," replied Peppers. "Ya, it's just his keys. Go forward again."

After a few seconds, Peppers yelled, "Stop. What's he doing now? He just put his hand under the truck. See? Right there," he said, as he pointed to the spot on the monitor.

"It looks like he's just balancing himself, trying to stand up," Frank said.

"Look closer. See his hand?"

"You're right. It's under the truck. But I didn't see anything in his hand when he bent down to pick up his keys," Frank commented. "Let me back it up a little."

"Right there. See, he pulled something out of his pocket." Peppers pointed once again to the monitor.

"Son of a bitch!" exclaimed Frank. "You're right. He just stuck a bomb under Freddie's truck. You got him!"

"Do you recognize him?" Peppers asked.

"I think so. I think he's been in the bar a couple of times."

"What about tonight?" Peppers asked excitedly. "Was he in here tonight?"

Frank thought for a second. "He was. I was talking to Freddie, and I wasn't paying much attention to the customers. But I remember that he was sitting way in the back, in a booth. I'm pretty sure he was alone. I can ask Pistol."

"I'll talk to Pistol," said Peppers.

"Well, he'll remember. He doesn't miss a thing that goes on here."

"I sure hope he has a name for me."

"If he ever heard it, he'll remember it," Frank told him.

"I take it he's a good bartender," Peppers remarked.

"He's the best. I'll tell you one thing about Pistol."

"What's that?"

"I'd never want to go up against him. People think Freddie is tough? Shit, he's nothing compared to Pistol. Pistol is one mean, lean fighting machine."

"Good to know," said Peppers. "You know

something, Frank?

"What?" Frank answered.

"I just realized that I have no idea what Pistol's real name is. I've never heard him called anything but Pistol."

Frank smiled. "His first name is Peter. He hates it, so don't ever call him that. His last name is Pistolli. That's where his nickname comes from."

"Well, that makes sense."

"Do you need anything else, Detective?"

"I'll need a copy of that video, Frank."

"No problem. I'll make a duplicate right now. You'll have it by the time you're ready to leave.

"Thanks," Peppers replied.

Detective Peppers walked over to where Pistol was standing behind the bar. "You got a minute?" he asked Pistol.

"Not really. We're pretty busy right now. Can it wait?"

Peppers shrugged. "I guess. I'll go talk to Demonti while I wait."

"He left," Pistol told him.

"He what?"

"He left right after you and Frank went into the office. He said he was tired and going home."

"What about his truck?"

"I don't know nothing about that, Detective. Did the video show anything?"

"Ya, it did. Do you . . ."

"Sorry. I'll be right back," Pistol said and walked down the bar to check on a customer who was waving at him.

Peppers waited a few minutes while Pistol served some customers their drinks. As Pistol walked towards the other end of the bar, he held out his hand, indicating that Pistol should stop. "I know you're busy, but take five. I need to talk to you. Now!"

Pistol hesitated. "Frank's office?" he asked after a couple of seconds.

"That's fine. Let's go."

Frank had been right about Pistol being observant. He had given Peppers a complete description of what the man looked like, right down to what color his socks had been.

Pistol told Peppers that it was the second time he had seen the man in the bar. He remembered that he had drank light beer and that he had sat in the same booth both times. He also told the detective that the man had paid with cash tonight but he was pretty sure that he had used a credit card when he had been in a few weeks back.

When Peppers asked for a copy of the credit card receipt, Pistol said that he would need to talk to Frank about that.

Frank told Peppers he would check the receipts and see if he could find a copy. But, it would have to wait until tomorrow, as he kept that information in a cabinet at his house.

Twenty minutes later, Detective Peppers was in his squad car, heading back to the station with a copy of the security video in his pocket.

He was done for the day but he wasn't ready to go home. He took his cell out of his pocket and made a call.

"You still up?"

He listened to Karlee mumble something unintelligible and smiled.

"Whatever. I'll be there in half an hour. I've got to stop by the station first."

Karlee closed her eyes, rolled over, and went back to sleep.

Chapter Thirty-two

"Are you okay?" Tony asked his brother, as he walked through the front door of Freddie's house.

Freddie looked up at him and muted the sound on his TV. "I'm fine. What the hell are you doing here at this late hour? Shouldn't you be out banging that girlfriend of yours?"

"I just heard about your truck. You didn't answer your cell and I was worried about you," Tony replied.

"I'm sorry. I'm just so tired of all this crap. Did you stop by the Squirrel House?"

"I did. I was looking for you."

"Is my truck still sitting out front?"

"It was when I got there but the towing company was getting ready to hook it up and tow it away. Where are they taking it anyway?"

"I think over to Jackson's Body Repair. The insurance guy can't take a look at it until Monday. So, now it's gonna sit there for a few days with me wondering if it can be fixed or not."

"I don't know, Freddie. From what I saw, it's probably totaled. It's a mess. My god, do you know how lucky you are that you weren't in it when that bomb went off?"

Freddie shrugged. "I guess. Maybe, it would have been better if I had been in it," he uttered.

"No way, Bro'. Don't even think that way. Hey, it's insured. Hopefully, the insurance company will total it and you'll get enough to buy another one."

"I don't think I'll get another one."

"What? You wouldn't replace it? I thought you loved that truck," Tony said.

"I do but I'd be better off in something that blends in. Every damn person in town knows that's me coming down the road."

"Well, that's true enough."

"I don't know what I'll do. I really liked driving it. That's one powerful piece of metal. Plus, it's bulletproof."

"Do you need a bulletproof tank, Freddie?"

Freddie shrugged. "You never know when someone you piss off might want to get even."

"Then, I guess you should quit pissing people off," Tony said, grinning.

"You want a drink?" Freddie asked.

"Naw. I'm good," Tony said.

"Are you sure? I have some Three Floyds Beer in the frig."

"Zombie Dust?" Tony asked, smiling.

"That's one of them," Freddie replied. "I've got a few Red Deaths, too."

"Twenty-two ounces is way too much for me. Unless you want to split one," Tony said.

"Let's do that."

"I need to ask you something," Tony said, as they walked into the kitchen.

"What's that?"

"I was wondering if you'd be my best man at my wedding."

Freddie stopped and turned to look at Tony, surprise written on his face. "You aren't seriously thinking about marrying that Campanale bitch, are you?"

"Watch the mouth, Freddie. You're talking about the woman I love."

"You gotta be fucking kidding me, Tony. What the hell? Why would you possibly want to marry her? You're getting it for free. Why the big rush to get married?"

"I know you and the Campanales have problems but if everyone would just sit down and talk, I think we could work them out."

Freddie looked at Tony, wondering how far he should go with this conversation. "Let me tell you something, Tony. There's a lot more going on than you realize. The Campanales are trying to kill me. I know it was one of them who tried to burn my house down. With me in it, if you recall. I'm also pretty sure it was one of them who bombed my car. I just can't prove it. Yet."

"Come on, Freddie. You don't know that for sure," Tony argued.

"Well, that's the thing. I do know for sure about the house. And, it's only a matter of time before Detective Peppers will have a positive ID on who planted the car bomb."

"How do you know who torched your house?" Tony asked.

"I have a video of the person who threw the bomb through my window."

"So, why haven't the police arrested him?"

"I haven't told the police about it. I'll take care of this my way."

"By doing what? Killing him?"

"It was a her, Tony. Not a him. The funny thing is that I decided yesterday to drop it. I was going to forget about the whole thing. Put it all behind me. But I'm sure as hell not putting anything behind me now. Not after tonight."

"I know for a fact that it wasn't Rebecca, so don't even go there."

"You're right. It wasn't Rebecca," Freddie replied. "However, if you blab any of this to Detective Peppers, I'll tell him who tried to blow me up. I'm afraid that wouldn't make Rebecca very happy. I'm gonna take care of this my way and there's nothing anyone can do about it. I haven't broken any laws yet, Tony, but the woman who tried to kill me sure as hell did."

"Come on, Freddie. You can't do this."

Freddie grinned. "Sure I can."

"Was it Karlee?" Tony asked, staring at Freddie. "It was her, wasn't it?"

"Not saying, Bro'."

"Emmy Lou?" Tony asked. "Naw, she doesn't have the balls. Plus, she's not a Campanale."

"Yet," Freddie said. "But she's practically one."

Tony picked up his glass of beer and finished it. "I'm leaving. I'm asking you to drop this, Freddie. For everyone's sake, including mine."

"So, when are you getting married," Freddie asked, changing the subject.

Tony was quiet for a few seconds. "Soon. Mike and Emmy Lou suddenly decided not to wait a year and to get married now. So, we all decided to make it easy on her folks and have a double wedding. It's not exactly what I hoped for but it's what Rebecca wants. It's not going to be anything fancy. We're just going to have a quiet ceremony with family and a few close friends. I was serious when I asked you to be my best man, Freddie. But if you don't drop this getting even idea, then maybe we should forget about it."

"You hardly know the woman, Tony. I just think

162

you're moving way too fast."

"I wouldn't know her at all if it wasn't for you. And, remember, she never called the cops on you."

"Only because of you," Freddie said.

"That's probably true."

"You know it's true," Freddie remarked.

"So, what do you say? Can you forget about them messing with your truck and be my best man?"

"I'll think about it. The thing is, though. . ."

"What?"

"Well, it's kind of out of my hands. If the police have a description of the person who planted the bomb under my truck, they'll go after him."

"Then, let's hope they don't," Tony said.

"Oh, you better hope they do. Because, if I find out who did it, it's not going to be pretty."

"Come on, Freddie," Tony whined. "Don't."

"They – blew – up – my – fucking - truck!" he yelled, emphasizing every word. "Don't you get it? They tried to kill me. As far as I'm concerned, they're already dead!"

"Well, then, fuck you, Freddie," Tony yelled back at his brother.

"Fuck you, too. Get the hell out of my house."

"Fine. I'm out of here."

"Fine," Freddie screamed. "Don't let the door hit you in the ass on the way out."

Chapter Thirty-three

They had prints but they didn't have any fingers to match them to. The Chicago Crime Scene Investigators had managed to get a couple of clean prints from Freddie's truck but after running them through the FBI Database, they came up empty.

Detective Peppers wished he could fingerprint Mike Campanale and his father, just to rule them out and put his mind at ease. But unless he had reasonable cause to get a warrant, he knew it wouldn't happen. He could ask them to volunteer to be fingerprinted but that might start a fight and getting into a battle with Karlee and her family is the last thing he wanted to happen.

He smiled when he thought about last night. He was amazed at how beautiful she had looked when she answered her door, messy hair and all. She had yawned in his face when he bent down to kiss her. She didn't say a word to him. She simply took his hand and led him into her bedroom, threw off the oversized t-shirt she was wearing, and proceeded to give him one of the most fantastic nights he could remember.

Peppers was positive that he was in love with Karlee and it scared him. Not the being in love part. He was more than ready for that. However, the possibility existed that someone in her family was trying to kill Freddie Demonti. Being the head investigator on that case could be a deal-breaker. What would happen to their relationship if the person who stuck that bomb under Freddie's car turned out to be Karlee's brother? Or, even her father. He hadn't ruled anyone out yet. Everyone was a suspect.

Peppers sat back in his chair and looked up at the

ceiling. My god, this place is filthy, he thought, as he noticed how yellow and stained the white ceiling tiles were. He opened his notebook and stared at it. I guess the first thing I should do is make a list of people who want Freddie dead, he thought, sighing deeply. He sat straight up again, picked up a pen, and started writing. The first name he wrote down was Mike Campanale.

Karlee was tired. She had crawled right back into bed after John left, planning on catching up on her sleep. However, the phone had rung and it was Rebecca telling her she was on her way over and asking her to put on a pot of coffee.

I wish I'd never answered that phone, she thought, as she listened to Rebecca ramble on about Tony and Firecracker getting into a fight.

"I'm telling you, Karlee, I've never seen Tony so upset. It's a good thing he can control his temper. He wanted to beat the crap out of him." Rebecca took a sip of her coffee and put the cup down on the coffee table. "He says Firecracker knows who tried to burn down his house."

Karlee looked over at her. Rebecca smiled. "Finally. I figured that would get your attention. I feel like I was talking to a wall for the last five minutes."

"He knows who it was?" Karlee said, obviously upset.

"That's what he told Tony. He knows and he's gonna get even."

"Who? Who did he say it was?" Karlee asked.

"He wouldn't tell him. He said it was a woman."

"It was a woman? How does he know?"

"He had a second security camera hidden in a

tree. The police don't know about it. I guess he saw her run to her car. He knows who the car belongs to."

"Damn it, Rebecca. This isn't good. What else did he tell Tony?"

"Freddie said he knew it wasn't me. Tony figures Firecracker thinks it was either you or Emmy Lou. And, he said Firecracker plans to get even."

Karlee frowned, shaking her head no. "No. It wasn't either one of us."

"Well, I figured it wasn't you. And, Emmy Lou is too chicken to do it. It has to be someone else that hates him enough to do something like that," Rebecca said. "The problem is, Karlee, he thinks it was one of us. I think we should tell John about this."

"We can't do that, Rebecca."

"Why not?"

Rebecca studied Karlee's face. "You know! You know who did it, don't you?" she exclaimed.

Karlee slouched back on the couch. "I can't say anything. I promised."

Rebecca stared at her sister. Finally, she said, "You've got to tell before Firecracker tries to kill you or Emmy Lou."

"I can't tell you. I'm sorry."

"I don't believe this. You know who blew up his truck, too. Don't you?"

"Not for sure," Karlee said, softly.

"You know what Tony told me?"

"What's that?" Karlee answered.

"Firecracker decided to put all that crap behind him. He decided to just let it go. I guess for Tony's sake. Whatever. But then someone – who you know – decided to blow him up. Now, he's ready to kill our whole family to get even."

Karlee looked away. "Then, I guess we'll just have to get him before that happens," she uttered.

"My god, Karlee, this has to end. We need to sit down with Firecracker and get this taken care of. This can't continue."

Karlee shrugged. "I don't know how – maybe..."

"What?"

"Do you think Tony could get Firecracker to meet with me?"

"I don't know. I mean, like – maybe he could. If he even wants to try. Tony can be stubborn, too." Rebecca suddenly realized what Karlee had said. "What did you mean? You said me, not us?"

"I know. I want to talk to him alone."

"You think you can work this out?" she finally said.

"I'd like to try."

"I'll talk to Tony," Rebecca told her. "I can't promise anything, though."

"That's all I can ask. Maybe, we could get together tomorrow morning, if Tony can work it out."

"Firecracker spends Sunday mornings with his mother. He takes her to church and then they usually go for brunch somewhere. It would have to be later in the day."

"You sure know a lot about his schedule. I don't care if it's morning or afternoon. Just see what you can do."

Rebecca stood up. "I'm meeting Tony in a little while for breakfast. I'll talk to him and get back to you."

Karlee shook her head in agreement. "Be careful, Sis."

Rebecca smiled at her. "Always am. Later."

"Love ya."

"Back atcha," Rebecca said and left.

Karlee sat back and put her feet up on the coffee table. She knew she had to make a phone call and she had no idea what she was going to say.

Chapter Thirty-four

"You're very beautiful," Freddie said.

"Thank you," Karlee replied.

Freddie waited, expecting her to return the compliment and tell him how handsome she thought he was. When Karlee remained silent, he looked over at Tony, who was sitting on the couch in his living room.

"What?" Tony asked, seeing the frown on Freddie's face. "Is something wrong?"

"No, nothing's wrong. Just forget it," Freddie said.

"Forget what? Did I miss something?"

"I said, forget it," Freddie snapped.

"I want to thank you for agreeing to meet with me, Mr. Demonti," Karlee said.

"Call me Freddie. We don't have to be so formal. I'll call you Karlee. Okay?"

"That's fine," Karlee replied.

"So, Karlee, what can I do for you on this beautiful Sunday afternoon? And, make it fast, will you? I have a golfing date."

"I appreciate your time," Karlee told him. "I'll try to be brief, so you can get out of here in time for your tee-off."

"How do you feel about Rebecca marrying into the Demonti family? Freddie asked, grinning.

Karlee glanced over at Tony and smiled. "I'm delighted. Tony makes my sister happy and that's all that matters."

Freddie looked at Tony. "Did you hear that, Tony? She's delighted. Isn't that wonderful?" he said, sarcastically.

"Knock it off, Freddie. We're not here to talk about

me and Rebecca," Tony said.

"In a way we are. I mean, if you think about it, I kind of hold your future in my hands, don't I?"

"Freddie, can we talk about that?" Karlee said. "Is there something we can do to make it right between our families? I know our family would like to see this all end peacefully."

Freddie stared at her and smirked. "Since when is trying to blow someone up peaceful? Do you also consider trying to burn my house down a peaceful act? You, your sister, and that other bitch that's going out with your brother is the reason I spent six months in jail. Emmy something or other is her name if I remember correctly. That's it, isn't it?"

Freddie waited for Karlee to answer him.

"Well?" he shouted at her.

"Yes," Karlee mumbled, obviously shook up at being yelled at.

"Damn right that's her name," Freddie yelled. "Now, you just want me to forget about everything and make peace? It's not that simple, lady. Stealing my tires and pulling that crappy prank in the park embarrassed the hell out of me."

"I'm really sorry. . ."

"Don't interrupt me."

"Sorry," Karlee murmured.

"If I hadn't left my keys on the bar Friday night, I'd be dead right now. If I had been sleeping when my house started on fire, I'd be dead right now. I'm only alive because of dumb luck and that isn't going to last forever. I don't just get over things, Karlee," Freddie said, his face turning red. "I get even!" he shouted.

Karlee looked away, afraid of what Freddie might

do next. She glanced over at Tony, hoping he would say something to calm Freddie down. Tony shook his head and looked away.

"He's not going to help you," Freddie said. "I only agreed to let him be here if he promised to keep his mouth shut. This is between us, Karlee. Isn't that right, Tony?"

Tony looked up. "That's right, Freddie," he replied.

"It seems to me that you're the only one doing all the talking," Karlee said, starting to get more pissed off than afraid. "I came here in good faith, hoping we could work this mess out, not to hear you rant. You wanna talk or not? Because I'm not gonna sit here and listen to your bullshit."

Freddie stared at her, not believing what she had just said. Suddenly, he laughed. "You got balls, lady. I've gotta give you that. Hey, Tony?"

"What?"

"If her sister is anything like this one, you're gonna have your hands full."

Tony grinned. "I already do."

Freddie looked at Karlee. "Okay," he said, "let's talk. You want a beer?"

Thirty minutes later, Karlee and Tony left Freddie's house, got in Tony's car, and drove away.

"Do you think he'll stick to it?" Karlee asked.

"He will as long as no one tries anything else. One thing about Freddie you should know. His word is gold. When he makes a promise, he keeps it. But if you cross him – well, it's not pretty."

"There's still one hitch, though."

"Peppers." Tony pointed out.

"Yes. If John identifies the man who planted that bomb, then this whole thing blows up."

"What are the chances of that happening?" Tony asked.

"Slim. At least, I think they are. However, you just never know these days with all the advanced technology and security cameras on every other street corner," Karlee replied.

"You're right about that," Tony agreed.

"You know, your brother can be pretty decent when he wants to be."

"I guess. He's not always a jerk. We were pretty close when we were kids. We don't have much in common anymore."

"Are you glad you moved to Cowtown?" Karlee asked.

"Are you kidding? I met your sister, didn't I? That was the best thing that ever happened to me."

"You know she told me how you met," Karlee said. "You and Freddie could both be in jail right now."

Tony smiled. "Like I said – best thing that ever happened to me. Besides, the fact that she didn't turn us in is one of the reasons that Freddie agreed to sit down and talk."

"You're a nice person, Tony. I'm glad it's worked out the way it has."

"What about you and John? Are you guys getting serious?"

Karlee grinned. "Could be. He's one hell of a nice guy."

"Ya," Tony said. "Too bad he's a cop."

Chapter Thirty-five

As soon as Tony dropped Karlee off at her house, she was on the phone informing her family that she had talked to Freddie and that they had agreed to a truce. At first, Mike was upset that Karlee had met with Freddie but when she told him that Tony had been with her, he calmed down.

"I hope this news helps Emmy Lou feel better. She's been so fixated on Demonti, it's ridiculous," Mike said.

"Well, she sure hasn't been herself lately," Karlee commented. "Is there something else going on with her?"

"Wedding jitters, I guess," Mike said.

"I suppose that can do it. Is she feeling any better? She said she thought she was coming down with the flu."

"Baby flu, maybe," Mike said.

Karlee let out a squeal. "Oh, my God, Mike. Is she pregnant?" she cried out.

"She thinks she might be but I honestly don't know."

"Well, have her take a test."

"She has, Karlee. She's taken a bunch of them. They all come back negative but she swears she's pregnant anyway. I'm not sure what's going on. The tests are negative but she hasn't had a period in a couple of months."

"Have you ever heard of a doctor, Mike? You better get her to one."

"I'm trying. Believe me, I'm trying. I don't know anyone who is more stubborn than she is."

"Just do it," Karlee said.

Karlee spent the next hour talking to the rest of her family, telling them about her meeting with Freddie, and trying to convince them that they could trust him to keep his word. The fact that Rebecca was marrying Tony helped Karlee's case and her family finally, although reluctantly, agreed to honor the truce.

Everyone breathed a little easier for the next few days.

On Wednesday morning, Freddie talked with his insurance agent about the damage to his truck. The agent told Freddie that he had contacted the company in Canada that had manufactured his vehicle. There was some – but not severe - body damage to the truck, but the damage to the inside of the car was extensive. The cost of transporting the truck back to Canada and repairing the damage would be more than the vehicle was worth. His truck was totaled.

Freddie decided to go shopping for a new vehicle. The new Bentley SUV looked promising, he decided, and the insurance payout would probably cover the cost. Plus, he figured he wouldn't stick out like a sore thumb, as he did when driving his truck.

Freddie couldn't help but feel a little sad about losing his truck. The more he thought about it, the harder it was trying to get over the fact that he would never be able to drive it again. Then, the very idea that he had to suck it up, because of some dumb truce he had made with that Campanale woman, started to weigh on him. The more Freddie thought about it, the madder he got.

At the same time that Freddie was talking to his insurance agent, Detective Peppers was looking at security videos that had come from the Dragon Lady Store and Milly's Beauty Parlor. Both stores were across the street from the Squirrel House Tavern, and the quality of both videos was excellent.

As Peppers watched one of the videos, he made notes on a yellow legal pad of paper. When the subject came into view and stood next to Freddie's truck, Peppers paused the video. He zoomed in to get a closer look at the face, determined that it definitely was a man, and yelled, "Jiggers, get over here, will ya?" at the ITT guy, who was sitting at his desk in the back of the room.

Jiggers got up from his desk and walked over to where Peppers was sitting. "What do you need, John?" he asked.

"See this face here on the monitor?"

"I do."

"Can you print out a close-up picture for me?"

"I can."

"Thanks," said Peppers

"Do you want me to run an ID search, too?" Jiggers asked.

"If you would, please."

"Will do."

"Thanks," Peppers said. "I appreciate it. When will I get it?"

"Tomorrow. I'm backed up."

Peppers looked up at him. "Everyone's backed up. I need it today."

"I'll do what I can," Jiggers told him.

She put her phone to her ear and listened to the man who was talking to her.

"I don't care what Karlee says. I don't trust him," she told him.

"Have you gotten any more messages from him?"

"No. But, that doesn't mean anything. I hadn't heard from him for a few days before this so-called truce happened. You know, that message where he threatened me. So, it wasn't the truce that made him stop texting me. I figure he's just waiting for the right time."

"The right time to do what?"

"To hurt me. What do you think?" she said.

"Let's not do anything now. Let's wait and see if everything quiets down."

"I don't trust him," she repeated.

"I know. Neither do I. We just have to be vigilant and keep watching our backs. In the meantime, we have to forget about doing anything else."

"You're comfortable with that?" she asked.

"For now. If we're lucky, he'll stick to his promise and this will all go away."

"God, I hope so. I'm so tired of being afraid. If not – well, I don't know what to do next. Have you been to the practice range yet?"

"I have."

"Well?"

"Well, what?"

"How did it go?" she asked.

"Let's just say I haven't killed one target yet."

Chapter Thirty-six

Detective Peppers glanced up at the wall clock and checked the time. It was already six-fifteen. He had a date with Karlee at seven, and he wanted to go home, shower, and change clothes before he picked her up. He knew he would never make it on time.

He picked up his cell phone and called her. The call immediately went to voice mail, which meant that she was probably talking to someone. He left a message telling her he would be late and headed towards the door. Just as he reached for the door handle, Jiggers yelled at him to wait.

Peppers turned as Jiggers walked towards him. "What's up?" Peppers asked him.

"I've got an ID on that man in the video," Jiggers told him. "You're probably gonna want to hear this before you leave."

"How'd you identify him?"

"We matched him to his driver's license in the DMV database. His name is Angelo Romano."

"I've never heard of him. Have you got an address for me?"

"Sure do. Are you going over there now?"

"Does he have a record?"

"Naw. Just a couple of traffic tickets from a few years ago. He's not dangerous," Jiggers told Peppers.

"He tried to blow someone up, Jiggers," Peppers said. "I'd say he's a little dangerous. He's gonna have to wait until morning, though. I have a date with Karlee and I'm already running late. I'll bring him in tomorrow. Put his information on my desk, will you?"

"You sure you don't want to send someone over to

pick him up tonight?" Jiggers inquired.

"No, I'll do it in the morning. He's not going anywhere. Thanks, Jiggers. Good work."

She read Freddie's text message for the second time. Her heart was beating so hard, that she thought she was going to have a heart attack. Truce, my ass, she thought. It hasn't even been a day and now he pulls this crap. I knew he couldn't be trusted.

She picked up her cell phone and made a call.

"What now?"

"We can't wait. It has to be tonight."

"Why? What changed since we last talked?"

"He sent me another text message. He said he's going to kill me and my entire family."

"Call the fucking police!"

"No! No police. Load your gun and meet me at Davies Park. By the bandstand."

"This is crazy. I don't know if I can shoot someone."

"You did in the war. You can do this."

"That was different."

"Then, I'll do it. But I'll need your gun. Meet me at nine by the bandstand."

"I seriously do not think this is a good idea."

"You don't have to stay. Just bring me the gun."

Detective Peppers checked himself out in the bathroom mirror and decided he looked just fine. He grinned at his reflection, thinking about how more important his appearance had become since he had met Karlee.

He picked up his phone and called her, wanting to

be sure she had listened to his voice message and knew he was going to be late.

"Hi, handsome," said Karlee, when she answered the phone.

"Hey, babe. Did you get my message?"

"I did. How long before you get here?"

"I'm leaving now. I should be there in about a half-hour. I can't wait to see you."

"Me, too. Drive safe," Karlee said and ended the call.

Jiggers sat back in his beat-up chair and stared at his computer monitor. Holy crap, he thought, this is not good. He looked at the time and decided he better go moving. He was supposed to meet his date in fifteen minutes and he'd be late if he didn't leave now. He sent Peppers a text asking him to call him as soon as possible and left the precinct.

Peppers felt the vibration of his phone in his pocket and made a mental note to check it later. Right now, he was walking up the front steps of Karlee's house, hoping she would answer the door in nothing but her birthday suit.

Freddie was just a little drunk and looking for a fight. He wanted to hurt someone. Bad.

He was pissed about his truck being blown up, his house being torched, spending six months in jail, and his tires being used as a planter. He was mad about everything bad that had ever happened to him. He wanted his truck back the way it was before it was set on fire. Most of all, he was mad at himself for ever agreeing to a truce with the fucking Campanales.

Freddie prided himself when it came to keeping his promises. He could not remember a time that he had broken a promise on purpose. Until now, that is. He had broken this one when he sent that text. He knew he shouldn't have sent it, telling her he was going to kill her and her family. Tough, he thought. I can't undo it now. I just need to watch my back and remember to take her phone, after I break her rotten little neck.

Freddie was about to order another beer, when his phone rang, letting him know that he had a text message. He checked it out.

"What the fuck!" he exclaimed.

Pistol glanced over at him. "Did you say something?" Pistol asked him.

Freddie looked up at the bartender and shook his head no. "Sorry. Just talking to myself."

He read through the message again and deleted it. He checked the time, ordered another beer, and waited.

Chapter Thirty-seven

"Well, that was fun," Karlee remarked.

"And, totally unexpected," Peppers said, grinning from ear to ear. "Do you still want to go out and eat?"

"What the hell, Peppers? Do you think you can jump into my bed, screw me, and get away without buying me dinner? I don't just give it away, you know. Of course, I want to go eat. Someplace nice, too."

Peppers laughed. "How about McDonalds?"

Karlee punched him playfully on the arm. I'm starving and that smart-ass remark just cost you a lobster dinner. How about you put your pants on so we can go eat?"

As Peppers reached for his pants, he remembered the call he'd received when he had arrived at Karlee's. He reached for his phone, read the text from Jiggers, and suddenly he felt sick to his stomach. "Crap," he mumbled softly.

Karlee glanced over at him. "Is something wrong? You look like your best friend just died."

"We've got a positive ID from the video. We know who put the bomb under Freddie's truck."

"Who was it? Anyone I know?"

John took Karlee's hand. "I have to leave, Karlee. I'm sorry."

"What's going on, John? Tell me."

"I can't. Not right now. I'm sorry."

Karlee didn't say anything. She watched John finish dressing. He bent down and kissed her cheek. "I'm so sorry. I'll call you later."

The minute Peppers was out her front door, Karlee picked up her phone and made a call.

"I'm on my way over," Karlee said.

"I'm on my way out. Some other time."

"No! You stay where you are. Whatever you do, do not leave your house. I need to talk to you and it has to be now," Karlee said.

"All right. I'll stay here. But this better be a matter of life or death, Karlee."

She ended the call and immediately checked the time. It was almost eight forty-five. Angelo wouldn't be there yet. They were supposed to meet at nine o'clock, but he was rarely on time. She had time to catch him before he showed up at the park. She hit a speed dial number and called his cell.

At eight-forty-five, Angelo Romano was waiting by the bandstand in Davies Park. He checked out the area. He wasn't surprised when he didn't see anyone else in the park. It was a cool Wednesday night, and it stood to reason that most people would be at home.

He heard footsteps and turned to see a man walking toward him. At first, Angelo didn't pay much attention, figuring it was just someone cutting through the park on their way home. Then, as the man got closer, Angelo recognized him. Afraid, he reached behind his back and pulled out a fully loaded Colt .45, which had been tucked into the back of his pants. However, before he realized what was happening, Freddie raised his arm and fired, hitting Angelo between the eyes, killing him instantly.

Freddie stood there and looked down at the man he had just killed. He kicked him hard in the ribs. "You stupid fuck. You think I'm so stupid I would just walk into your fucking trap?" he whispered to the dead man.

Freddie turned around and started to leave. As he heard a phone ring, he hesitated. He reached down and took Angelo's phone out of his pocket. Freddie glanced at the .45 lying on the ground, picked it up, and put it in his jacket pocket. Turning Angelo slightly to one side, he reached into Angelo's back pocket, took out his wallet, and walked away.

Detective Peppers was on his way to Angelo Romano's house when heard the call over his radio. The dispatcher said that an unidentified male had been shot and killed in Davies Park. Any cops near that area were to report immediately. Peppers hit the lights and siren and headed to the park.

Less than five minutes later, Peppers was standing at the feet of Angelo Romano, talking to the cop who was the first responder on the scene.

"You haven't touched anything, right?" Peppers asked.

"He's exactly like I found him."

Peppers looked at the cop's badge. "What's your first name, Miller?"

"Jack."

"Okay, Jack. Has the coroner been called?"

"He's on his way, Detective."

"Who found him?" Peppers asked Miller.

"That kid standing over there." Miller turned, pointed, and noticed that the kid was sitting on the grass. "Well, he's sitting right now. He doesn't look too well."

"It's a hard thing to find a dead body. There may not be much of a hole in the front but the back of his skull is blown out. There's a lot of blood. It can make anyone queasy."

"It sure can," Miller agreed. "I'll never forget my first one."

"It's something you never forget."

"This is probably just a robbery gone bad," Miller said. "Guy probably didn't want to give it up."

"I don't think so. Not this time," Peppers told him. "I know who this guy is."

"You knew him? Man, that's rough," Miller remarked.

"No. I didn't know him. I just know who he is – ah, was. He's a person of interest in a crime I'm investigating. I was gonna pull him in tomorrow morning. He's been identified as the guy that planted the bomb under Freddie Demonti's truck."

"You're kidding? Man, that's tough. Too bad you didn't pick him up today. He'd still be alive and safe, sitting in a jail cell."

Peppers remained quiet, thinking about what Miller had just said. "Damn, you're probably right," he finally said, softly.

"What does this do to your case?" Miller asked him.

"It makes it a whole lot tougher, Miller. Believe me, this hurts in more ways than you can imagine."

Chapter Thirty-eight

Freddie turned off his SUV and stared out the window. He thought about the fact that he had just killed a man and was feeling nothing. The anger that had preceded the shooting was gone but that wasn't new. Freddie had killed before in anger and he always experienced this lack of emotion afterward.

He got out of his vehicle and walked to the back door of his pawnshop. He unlocked the door and went down a short hall to his office.

He removed the disk from the DVD player, which had recorded the time he entered the back of the building, and replaced it with a blank one. He broke the one that he had removed in half and put the two pieces in his pocket.

Freddie walked over to a filing cabinet and opened it. He took out a bottle of scotch and poured himself a drink. He sat down behind his desk and flipped a switch on the intercom. "Steve, my office," he said, loudly.

He waited. As soon as he heard the knock on his door, he told Steve to come in.

"Freddie, I didn't know you were here," Steve said. "What's up?"

"I had some paperwork I needed to get done. How's business tonight?"

"Man, we've been busy. I haven't even had time for a piss break."

"How's the new guy working out?" Freddie asked.

"He seems to be doing okay. He catches on pretty quick." Steve gave him an inquiring look. "How long have you been here, anyway? You usually check in at the front when you get here."

Freddie looked at his watch. It was almost nine-thirty. "I got here a little before nine. I glanced up front when I got here but you were busy. I wanted to get at these invoices and get out of here. Do you need anything before I leave?"

"Nope. We're good," Steve told him.

"By the way, has anyone pawned any guns this week?"

Steve thought for a few seconds. "I think there were a few. I'll get the log if you want to look at it."

"No. I'm good. Just wondering, that's all."

"Anything else, Boss?"

"That's it. I'm gonna finish up and, then, I'm out of here."

Freddie finished his drink and poured himself a second one. He wanted to kill a little more time before he drove back to Cowtown.

It was a little after midnight when Karlee ended the call from Peppers. Angelo Romano was dead. Peppers said he was on his way over to inform Angelo's wife and he thought Karlee might like to call Mike and Rebecca to give them the bad news.

Karlee immediately called Mike and asked him to come over. "Do you know what time it is?" Mike whined. "What's so important it can't wait until morning?"

"Angelo's dead, Mike. And, we need to talk. Now. Not tomorrow. This is important."

"What the hell do you mean, Angelo is dead? What happened?"

"He was murdered. Shot."

"What the hell are you talking about? Angelo murdered? What the hell is going on, Karlee?"

186

"Just get your ass over here!" she yelled. "Sorry. I'm sorry I yelled," she immediately told him. "Please, Mike. Just get over here."

"I'll be there in a few minutes."

As soon as Karlee hung up with Mike, she called Rebecca, asking her to come over as soon as possible.

"Tony's coming with me," Rebecca told her.

"I don't know if that's a good idea," Karlee said.

"I don't really care. He's coming with."

"Whatever, Rebecca. I'm too tired to fight. Just get over here, please."

An hour later, Karlee sat back in her chair, and let out a deep sigh. "That's it," she told Mike, Rebecca, and Tony. "That's what's been going on. I'm sorry I kept you out of the loop but I promised not to say anything. However, after what happened tonight, I thought you should all know."

"Unbelievable," Rebecca said. "I can understand – well, kind of – about torching Firecracker's house and trying to get even with what he did to Mike. What I don't understand is how she got Angelo involved. This is all crazy."

"Does Peppers think it was Firecracker who shot Angelo?" Mike asked Karlee.

"I honestly don't know what he thinks. All I know is that we've got to do everything we can to protect her," Karlee replied.

"How do we do that? Eventually, it's bound to come out that she threw that bomb through his window."

"Not if we keep our mouths shut and play dumb," Karlee exclaimed. "We know nothing. Get it!"

"Are you going to be able to do that, Karlee?" Mike asked. "You're dating the cop who's investigating this shit."

"You think I don't know that?" Karlee said. "I know how to keep my mouth shut. Don't worry. Just be sure you guys do the same. We're going to get through this."

Rebecca glanced over at Tony. "What are you going to do if it was Firecracker who shot him?"

Tony shrugged. "It wouldn't surprise me if Freddie did shoot him. If he found out that Angelo put that bomb under his truck, he would have been furious."

"But we had just made a truce, Tony. You told me that he would keep his word and we didn't have to worry. Why would he break the truce?" Karlee asked.

"Why? I don't know. Maybe, he got drunk and something set him off. I don't understand him and I certainly can't explain him."

Mike stood up. "I've got to get back to Emmy Lou. So, we're all agreed, then. We know nothing. You okay with that, Tony?"

Tony shook his head yes. "I'm good."

"Alright, everyone. Out. Go home, and try to get some sleep," Karlee said.

"What about Mom and Dad? Who's going to tell them about Angelo?" Mike inquired.

"I already did," Karlee told him. "I talked to them after I called you guys. I'm going over there first thing in the morning."

"So, Dad knows about all this, too?" Rebecca asked.

"He does. I told him everything."

"How did he take it?"

"How do you think?" Karlee replied.

Chapter Thirty-nine

Rebecca was unusually quiet after they left Karlee's house. When Tony tried to discuss what had happened to Angelo, she softly asked him not to talk. "I just want to go home," she had said.

They spent a restless night wrapped in each other arms. Every time Tony moved away, Rebecca pulled him closer to her, needing the warmth of his body next to her.

He woke early, needing to use the washroom, and left her bed. A few minutes later, he was back by her side, holding her as she wept.

It was the first time Tony had seen Rebecca cry and he realized that she was more fragile than he thought.

"I'm so sorry, babe. I know losing Angelo is rough. Your family is going through a lot right now."

"That's not why I'm crying," Rebecca told him, still crying.

"It's not?"

"No. I'm afraid I'm going to lose you. I don't know how I could go on without you. Please don't leave me."

Tony pulled back in surprise and looked at her. "Why would you lose me? I love you, Rebecca. You know that."

"And, I love you, too. But, what's going to happen to us if your brother killed Angelo?"

Tony wiped a tear from her cheek and kissed her. "Nothing is going to change. You are all I want. Whatever Freddie did or didn't do isn't going to change a thing between us."

"Do you still want to marry me?"

Tony smiled. "More than anything."

Rebecca draped her arms around Tony's neck and pulled him closer to her. "Kiss me," she whispered.

"How about you take those ugly pajamas off first?"

"They aren't ugly. Besides, they keep me nice and warm."

"That's what I'm here for," Tony said, as he reached down towards her ankles, grabbed her pajama bottoms, and pulled them off. "You don't need no stinkin' jamas," he said, laughing as she squealed.

After Mike left Karlee's, he decided to wait and have a long talk with Emmy Lou in the morning. It was late, she hadn't been feeling well when he left the house, and he didn't want to wake her.

He had been as quiet as possible when he got home, had undressed in the dark, and managed to slip into bed without waking Emmy Lou. He was mentally exhausted, trying to absorb what Karlee had told him. It didn't take but a minute, before he was asleep and snoring.

Mike woke early, surprised that Emmy Lou was already up. He got up, used the washroom, and went to the kitchen, expecting to see her drinking a cup of coffee and reading the morning newspaper.

What he found was a note on the kitchen table. He opened it.

Mike, I'm going away for a few days. I need some time to myself to sort things out. Everything seems to be spinning around and there are days that I feel like I'm going crazy. Please don't worry about me. I'm sorry. I love you. Emmy Lou.

Mike stood there, stunned and trying to absorb

what he had just read. Emmy Lou was gone.

"You want another cup of coffee?" Victor Campanale asked his daughter. "Why aren't you working this morning?"

"No, thanks. I've had enough coffee. I do have to get going, though. I have some things I need to do. Thanks for the ear, Dad."

"No problem. I doubt I was much help, though."

"You were. I thought if John knew what really happened, he'd go easy on her," Karlee told her father.

"It doesn't work that way, Karlee. He's a cop first. Besides, it isn't up to him to make that decision."

"Then, I won't say anything, and I'll let the cards fall where they may."

"That would be for the best. Right now, we've got Angelo's funeral to worry about."

"I know. I just think she's more important right now than Angelo?"

"Of course, she is. However, there's a good possibility that no one will ever find out it was her that tried to burn that house down."

"A very slight possibility, Dad. I just think it would be easier on her if she turned herself in."

"Absolutely not!" Victor shouted. "It's best if you stay out of it, Karlee. I mean it."

"Stay out of it? How do I do that? I'm so deep into it, I'll never get out."

"Let's just wait and see what happens. Please."

"Alright, Dad. I hope you're right about this," Karlee said.

Peppers had called it a night around two-thirty

and headed home. He had been tempted to stop by Karlee's to see how she was doing but thought better of it, knowing he would see her later in the day.

After a few hours of sleep, Peppers was back at his office, looking over the reports handed in by Officer Miller and the kid that had found Romano's body.

Perhaps Officer Miller was right, Peppers considered after reading his report. The fact that Romano's wallet and phone were missing could be an indication that it was a robbery gone bad. However, Pepper's gut told him differently and his gut was usually right.

He checked the time, saw that it was almost seven a.m., and decided to go talk to Freddie Demonti. He knew Freddie wouldn't be happy about being awakened that early. However, Peppers figured if it was Freddie who had done the shooting, the sooner he talked to him the better.

Freddie didn't hear the doorbell. However, the pounding on his front door did the trick and woke him up. Freddie reached for his pants, pulled them on, and went downstairs to answer the door. He was pissed about having been disturbed after only a few hours of sleep. He had a horrible headache and the light bothered his eyes.

He pulled open the door, ready for battle. He managed to stop himself before he yelled out any threats to do bodily harm to the person who had the gall to wake him up.

Detective Peppers was standing in the doorway with two containers of hot coffee in his hands, smiling.

Freddie sighed. "What the fuck, Detective. Can't a

man get a few hours of sleep anymore?"

Peppers grinned. "Good morning, to you, too, Freddie. It's a beautiful day. The sun is shining but, unfortunately, not all is right with the world. We need to talk. Coffee?" he asked, as he handed Freddie one of the cups and brushed by him, as he entered Freddie's house.

"Can't it wait?" Freddie whined.

"Nope. Not today, it can't. Let's sit. You and I are going to have a conversation."

Freddie sat down across from Peppers and waited. After a few seconds, he took the lid off his coffee and took a sip. "Good coffee. Dunkin' Donuts?"

"That's what it says on the container," Peppers answered. "If you opened your eyes, you could see it for yourself."

Freddie sighed deeply. "What do you want now?"

"Where were you last night, Freddie?"

"Haven't we had this conversation before, Peppers?"

"Might have. So, where were you?"

Freddie sat back in his chair, took another sip of coffee, and burped. "Sorry. Let's see. You want to know what I did last night. All night?"

"Where were you from – let's say, from eight until midnight?

"Well, first, I started at the Squirrel House."

"What time?"

"I guess around seven-thirty or so."

"Then, what?"

"I left around eight-thirty and drove over to the shop. I did some paperwork and left around ten."

"Can someone verify the time?" Peppers asked.

"I would think so. Talk to Steve, my night manager. He'll tell you I was there."

"What did you do after you left the pawnshop?"

"I went to a strip club, got me a couple of lap dances, got shit-faced, came home, and fell into bed. Where, by the way, I would still be if you hadn't come pounding on my door."

"What strip club?"

"I don't know. The one on Montana Street."

"There's probably a dozen strip clubs on Montana. You don't remember the name of the one you visited?"

"No, Peppers, I don't." Freddie frowned. "Wait a minute. Why the hell are you asking me all these questions?" he asked Peppers.

"I wondered when your brain was going to start working. Do you know Angelo Romano?"

Freddie thought for a minute. "Sorry, I've never heard of him. Why? What did he do?"

"He went and got himself killed last night. That's what he did."

"What the fuck does that have to do with me? I don't even know the guy."

"Well, he sure knew you. He knew you well enough to want to kill you, Freddie. He's the guy that planted the bomb under your truck. You sure you don't know him?"

"Maybe he owes me money. I'll check that out, but I sure don't recognize his name."

"You do that," Peppers replied. "In the meantime, I'll check out your story about where you were last night."

"Be my guest," Freddie told him. "I've got nothing to hide."

Peppers stood up and walked towards the front door. He turned and looked back at Freddie, who was still sitting in his chair. "By the way, who called you around eight o'clock last night?"

"I didn't get no call," Freddie said.

"Sure you did. Pistol remembers you getting a call. He said you acted upset afterward."

Freddie shook his head. "Nope. It doesn't ring a bell. Pistol must be mistaken."

"You want to let me check your phone? Maybe you just forgot."

"You want to show me a warrant?" Freddie responded, getting aggravated.

Peppers smiled. "See you later, Freddie," he said and left.

Freddie picked up his container of coffee and threw it across the room.

Chapter Forty

Detective Peppers drove back to the precinct after he left Freddie's house. He had received a message that a possible witness in the Romano shooting had surfaced, and he should get back to the station as soon as possible. Peppers figured it would probably be a dead-end but you never ignored information that might be vital to a case.

He noticed a young boy, around sixteen or seventeen years of age, sitting on a chair next to his desk. Peppers frowned, knowing if this was his witness, anything the kid had to say would probably be useless. He walked over to his desk and held out his hand. The teenager shook it and smiled nervously.

"I hear you've got some news for me," Peppers said as he sat down behind his desk.

"I think so, sir."

"What's your name, son?" Peppers inquired.

"Brad. Brad Samuels, sir."

"It's good to meet you, Brad. And, you don't need to call me sir. Detective or John will do fine."

"Okay, Detective," Brad said.

"So, what have you got for me, Brad?"

"I saw the man who shot that guy in the park last night."

Peppers stared at Brad. "You saw the shooting?"

"Yes, sir. Me and my friend."

"Really? Do you think you would recognize this man if you saw him again?"

"Sure. Everyone knows him."

"Knows who?"

"That guy they call Firecracker. Everybody around

here knows him and that big ass truck he drives."

"Not anymore," Peppers muttered.

"What?" Brad asked.

"He doesn't drive it anymore."

"He doesn't?" Brad asked, nervously.

"Did you see him driving it last night, Brad?" Peppers asked,

"No. Not last night. But I saw him in the park. What happened to his truck?"

"Somebody blew it up," Peppers informed him.

"No shit!" Brad said and started to turn red in the face. "Sorry, sir. I didn't mean to swear."

"Don't worry about it. Alright, Brad. Let's start from the beginning and you tell me everything you saw and did last night."

"Me and my friend..."

"What's your friend's name?" Peppers interrupted.

"I promised not to tell."

"Well, you might have to tell us sometime."

"I promised."

"Go on," Peppers said.

"Well, me and my friend were cutting through the park last night and..."

"What time was that?"

Brad looked at Peppers, obviously getting upset with all the interruptions. "I guess it was around eight-thirty or so. Maybe, it was closer to nine o'clock. I'm not exactly sure. Anyway, we were cutting through the park and we were on the west side of the bandstand when we decided to light up. We sat down on a bench and that's when we heard..."

"Light up what?" Peppers interrupted.

"What?" Brad said.

"What were you lighting up?"

"A cigarette. Okay?"

"Go on," Peppers said.

"Anyway, we heard some footsteps, so we looked over and saw a man on the other side of the bandstand. He just stood there, looking around. Like, you know, he was waiting for someone."

"Then what?" Peppers asked.

"Nothing. He didn't do nothing for a few minutes. Then, we heard some more footsteps, so we looked over at him again. That's when we saw Firecracker shoot the man. He walked right up to him and shot him in the head. Then, he walked away."

"Is that all you saw?" Pepper asked.

"I guess. No. Wait. He turned and bent down like he was picking something up off the ground."

"And, you're sure you recognized the shooter?"

"Ya. I said it was Firecracker. But he might have been defending himself, you know. Like, it might have been self-defense."

"What makes you think that?" Peppers asked, not sure what the kid was getting at.

"The first guy had a gun, too. He pulled it out as Firecracker walked toward him."

Peppers stared at the kid. "You saw him with a gun? Are you sure? It's pretty dark in the park at night."

"Not where the guy was. There's a lot of light around the bandstand. I'm pretty positive it was a gun."

"Could it have been a cell phone that you saw?"

Brad thought for a second. "I guess. But we both thought it was a gun."

"What did you do then?" Peppers inquired.

"We ducked down so the guy wouldn't see us. As

soon as the guy left, we took off."

"You took off? That's not good, Brad. Why didn't you call the police?"

Brad looked away. "We were afraid," he told Peppers.

"Afraid of what? Afraid that the guy saw you?"

Brad hesitated before he answered. "Not that."

"Then why'd you run?"

"I guess we didn't want to get involved."

"Or, is it possible that it wasn't a regular cigarette that you were smoking? Maybe, it was a joint?"

"Maybe," said Brad. "But my friend and I talked about it later and decided that we should tell you guys what we saw."

"How old are you, Brad?"

"Sixteen and a half."

"Is your friend older than you?"

"I guess."

"And he provided the joint, right?"

Brad slouched down in the chair. "I guess."

"And that's why he made you promise not to tell us his name."

Brad didn't say anything.

"Right?" Peppers asked.

"I guess," he mumbled. He looked up at Peppers and frowned. "Am I in trouble? Because, you know, I was just trying to help."

Peppers smiled at him. "You're not in any trouble, Brad. I wish there were more good citizens like you."

Brad smiled and sighed with relief. "Man, you had me worried there for a minute."

Peppers reached into a desk drawer and pulled out a pad of yellow paper. He picked up a pen and stood up. "Come with me," he told Brad.

"Where are we going?"

"I'm gonna take you into a room that's quiet, where you won't be interrupted. I want you to write down everything you just told me."

"Just like in the movies, right?" Brad asked.

"Right. Just like in the movies."

"Is my mom here, yet?" Brad asked.

"You called your mom?"

"Ya. I figured she should know where I am."

"I'll check to see if she's here. You just write. I'll be back in a few minutes."

Peppers walked out of the room and fist-punched the air. "Yes," he exclaimed, excitedly. "You're mine now, Demonti!"

Chapter Forty-one

Freddie wasn't at home when Detective Peppers arrived with a search warrant. After what Peppers thought was a significant number of doorbell rings and knocks on the front door, he turned to the three cops standing behind him. "Do it," he told them It took less than two minutes to jimmy the lock and they were in Freddie's house.

He gave instructions to the policemen to search the house from top to bottom. Although they were looking for a gun, the warrant was broad enough to include any other items that could be connected to their case. Peppers looked around for a computer but did not find one. He probably has a laptop and carries it with him, Peppers thought.

As soon as the search was underway at Freddie's house, Peppers took off and headed to the pawnshop. He had sent three police officers there, who were tearing the pawnshop apart, looking for the murder weapon.

One of the cops had contacted Peppers and told him that Freddie had become furious when he handed him the warrant and had taken a swing at him. Freddie was now handcuffed to a chair in his office, outraged and threatening to kill every cop in Chicago. Peppers couldn't wait to get there.

"What the fuck do you think you're doing, Peppers?" Freddie screamed when Peppers walked into Freddie's office. "I'll have your badge for this. By the time I'm done with you, you won't have a pot to piss in. I'm suing you and the City of Chicago. This is downright harassment. You haven't got any cause to do this."

Peppers smiled at him. "Sure I do, Freddie."

"What's so fucking funny? Take these cuffs off me. They're too damn tight."

"I'll uncuff you from that chair when I get ready to leave. Then, I'll put those cuffs right back on you and take you for a ride to the station. I hear you took a swing at one of my boys. That wasn't very nice of you. Now, I can add assaulting a police officer to my list of charges against you."

Freddie glared at him. "Big deal. So, you got me on attempting to hit a cop."

"It is a big deal," Peppers said.

"I didn't hit him. You have nothing."

"But you tried, and that's enough."

Freddie got a puzzled look on his face. "What do you mean, list of charges?"

Hearing his name being called, Peppers turned towards the office door and saw one of his officers standing there.

"What do you need?" Peppers asked him.

"There are at least fifty – maybe more - guns here. You want we should bag them all?"

"We're looking for a .38. You can rule out the shotguns and the antique shit. If you think we should check all of them, then, by all means, bag all of them. Use your judgment."

"Will do," the officer replied and walked back into the store.

"You're looking for a gun? What the hell for?"

"It always helps to make our case a little stronger if we can find the murder weapon. But in your case, Freddie, we don't need it."

"What the fuck do you mean – my case? What

case is that?"

Peppers locked eyes with Freddie. "Why, your murder case, Freddie. I got you! Your money isn't going to buy you out of this one."

Freddie looked shocked. "I didn't kill nobody! What the hell are you talking about?"

Peppers smiled. "We have an eyewitness who saw you shoot Angelo Romano."

Freddie stared at him. "I want to call my attorney," Freddie said, his face turning red. "Now!"

"I just bet you do," Peppers said.

Brad Samuel picked Freddie out of a lineup as the man he saw shoot Angelo Romano. Freddie was arrested, read his rights, and placed in an interrogation room. Peppers made him wait an hour before he finally went in to talk to him.

"I want my lawyer. I have the right to make a call."

"You certainly do. I was just wondering if you'd like to confess before you do that? It would make things so much easier, Freddie."

"Lawyer."

"Why'd you kill him?"

"L A W Y E R," Freddie spelled out. "Now!"

"We have a positive ID."

"An ID for what?" Freddie yelled. "I didn't do anything. How many times do I have to tell you?"

"Actually, there were two people who saw you shoot Romano. You might as well tell us why you did it."

Freddie gave Peppers a dirty look and remained silent.

Peppers handed his cell phone to Freddie. "Here. Make your call."

"I'd like you to leave the room," he told Peppers.

"And, I'd like to be rich enough to retire, so I don't have to deal with scumbags like you every day. Make your call or give me my phone back."

Freddie hesitated; then, he picked up the phone and made a call.

Peppers killed time catching up on paperwork, while he waited for Freddie's lawyer to show up. He had been tempted to throw Freddie in the cage but decided to let him stay where he was, without anyone to talk to.

Freddie's lawyer, Bobby Martinelli, showed up an hour and fifteen minutes after Freddie had called him, looking disheveled and out of breath. As Peppers showed him to the room where Freddie was waiting, he mentioned to Martinelli that they had a rock-solid case against Freddie.

"You cops always say that," Martinelli replied.

"We have a couple of eyewitnesses who saw him do the shooting. He's going down, Martinelli. It's just a matter of how long. You might want to try to get him to cooperate. He might get a lighter sentence."

"You can't promise that."

"No, but the DA can. He's on his way down here right now. He'll cut a deal if you can get Freddie to confess."

Martinelli stared at Peppers. "Are you serious? You really have eyewitnesses?"

"Damned right I do," Peppers replied. "See if you can get him to talk."

"I'll talk to him but I doubt he'll go for it. He's a stubborn bastard."

"That he is," Peppers agreed and watched as

Martinelli walked into the interrogation room to talk to his client.

An hour later, Martinelli opened the door and waved at Peppers, who was sitting at his desk.

Peppers got up and walked over to him. "What's up?" he asked.

"Where's the DA?"

"He went for coffee. You need him?"

"Yep. Freddie's ready to cut a deal."

"No shit?" Peppers said, totally surprised. "I'll get him for you."

Peppers started to walk away, then, turned and asked Martinelli, "What changed Freddie's mind?"

"He knows he's in big trouble this time. Plus, he's got information to trade. He figures if he helps you close a couple of open cases, the DA will cut him some slack."

Peppers shook his head. "I will never figure out what makes people tick. Demonti is the last person I thought would cut a deal."

Chapter Forty-Two

Immediately after Freddie reached an agreement with the DA, Peppers called Karlee and told her he was on his way over. Thirty minutes later, the two of them were sitting at her kitchen table, drinking a beer.

"Who died?" she said, staring at the somber look on Peppers' face. "Sorry. Under the circumstances, I guess that wasn't called for. But something's the matter. What it is, John?"

He looked at her, a painful expression covering his face. "I don't know how to tell you this. In fact, I shouldn't be telling you this. But I figure you'd never forgive me if you heard it from someone else."

"You're scaring the crap out of me," Karlee said. "What's going on?"

"We arrested Freddie Demonti for the murder of your Uncle Angelo a few hours ago. He cut a deal with the DA, Karlee. He gave up some people and tied them to some of our open cases, including his house being bombed."

"Are you saying you know who did it?"

"We do. Once Freddie started talking, we couldn't shut him up. He told us that he has a video of the person that tried to burn his house down."

"So, he knew all along who it was?"

"That's what he said. He also told us that he figured it was Angelo that tried to kill him by blowing up his truck. He was right about that."

"I still find that so hard to believe," Karlee commented.

"Freddie got a text Wednesday night asking him to come to Davies Park at nine-thirty. He figured it was a setup, got there early, and found Angelo waiting for him. Angelo pulled a gun and Freddie shot him. He's claiming he killed Angelo in self-defense. He might be telling the truth. There was a kid who saw the shooting and he said Freddie didn't fire his gun until after Angelo pulled a gun on him. The thing is, though – well, the text came from a woman, Karlee."

Karlee looked at him, concern written all over her face. "Do you know who it was?" she asked.

"I do. What I don't know, Karlee, is if you were possibly involved in some way?"

Karlee looked shocked that Peppers would ask such a question. "Of course not," she exclaimed. "How could you think that?"

"I'm sorry I had to ask you that." He hesitated a moment. "You know who it was, don't you?"

"Rebecca told me but I don't believe it."

"It's true. I'm sorry you found out that way."

"What's going to happen to her?" she asked, as tears started to run down her cheeks.

Peppers got up from the table, walked over to her, put his arms around her, and held her. "She's being arrested right now."

"John, please. Can't you do something?"

"I can't. It's not my case or my call. It pains me to say this but I think her best bet would be an insanity plea."

"You think she's nuts?" Karlee said.

"I didn't say that. She might have been temporarily insane. It's obvious she was scared to death that something was going to happen to her. I guess, in her own way, she thought she had to protect herself and her family. And, she had every right to be scared. I'm positive that if she had been in the park with Angelo, Freddie would have shot her, too."

"Or, they might have killed Freddie," Karlee added. "That's a possibility, too, isn't it?"

"It is. After all, Freddie was sending her threatening texts, saying he was going to kill her and her family," Peppers said.

"He threatened to have her gang-raped, too," Karlee said.

Peppers let go of her and took a step back. "How do you know that?" He stared at her. "My God, I don't believe it! You already know all of this, don't you? You know everything I'm telling you. What the hell, Karlee? What else have you been lying about?"

Karlee wiped the tears from her cheek with the back of her hand. "I'm sorry. I promised not to say anything."

"I thought you trusted me,"

"I do. I do trust you," Karlee uttered.

"But obviously, not enough." John looked Karlee in the eyes. "Who else knows? Your whole family? Am I the only one that's been kept in the dark?"

"John, please, don't be angry. Let me explain."

Peppers stared at her. "I shouldn't be angry? Do you seriously think I could ever trust you after this? There's nothing you can say that is going to make this right. You've played me right from the beginning, haven't you Karlee? I can't believe that I've been such a fool. Is anything you've told me the truth?"

Karlee reached for John's hand. "John, please. I love you. What can I do?"

John pulled his hand away. "I don't believe you." He stepped further away from her, his emotions getting the best of him. "I can't do this..."

"What are you going to do?"

Peppers stared at her. "I'm not going to do a damned thing. I'm off this case because of my involvement with you."

"What's going to happen to her?"

"Right now, Karlee, I don't give a damn what happens to her or you and your fucked up family."

John turned and walked towards the door.

"Please, don't go," Karlee sobbed.

John turned and stared at her. "You really don't get it, do you?"

Karlee looked confused. "Get what? What did I do that's so horrible?"

"Goodbye, Karlee," John said, his voice breaking with emotion.

Karlee stood in the doorway, tears running down her cheeks, as she watched John walk towards his car. Suddenly, she yelled, "John! Wait!"

John turned and looked at her. "What?"

"Please, tell me."

He shook his head. "Tell you what? There's nothing left to say."

"Tell me. What would you have done if it had been your mother?"

Chapter Forty-three

"What's up, Karlee," Mike asked his sister.

"Turn on your television. Now!" she exclaimed.

"What's going..."

"Just do it. Channel four. I think I just saw Emmy Lou on TV."

Mike switched on his television and flipped to channel four. He stared at the picture for a moment, shocked. "It is her. My God, Karlee, I haven't heard from her in months. What's she doing at the courthouse?"

"The verdict is in. He was found not guilty."

"No way."

"Wait. Freddie is coming out of the courthouse. Oh, my God, look at that smug look on his face."

Freddie stood on the top step of the courthouse and looked around. "That's a hell of a crowd. Looks like all the newspapers are here," he murmured to his lawyer, who was standing next to him.

"Don't say anything, Freddie."

"Mr. Demonti, do you think this was a fair verdict? After all, there were eyewitnesses to the shooting," a reporter yelled.

Freddie pulled out a big cigar and bit down on it. He pulled out a lighter and lit up. "Made-up eyewitnesses, you mean, he replied, blowing out smoke. "If they were real, why didn't they testify? Where are they?" he said grinning. "I had nothing to do with that guy's death. Justice was done here today."

"But you confessed to killing him," another man cried out.

"Word is that you paid them off," a reporter yelled.

"That's bullshit. There never were any real witnesses. The cops lied to me. Told me that someone saw me kill that guy. A bunch of crap. I didn't even know him. Why would I kill him? The cops had been harassing me for weeks before all this happened. I had reached the point where I couldn't handle it anymore. I was about ready to have a nervous breakdown. I would have confessed to killing Jimmy Hoffa just to get them off my back."

"How does it feel to be out after all these months?"

"Great! It's fucking great."

"What are your plans now?" another reporter shouted.

"I plan to go home and soak in a hot tub for a few hours. Then, I'm gonna go have a few beers at The Squirrel House Tavern – the best damn tavern in..." He stopped talking as he saw a familiar woman in the crowd watching him. "Sorry, I've got to get going. My mother is waiting to take me home," he told the reporters, suddenly stopping the interview.

"Mr. Demonti, one more question."

"Sorry, guys. That's it, for now," Freddie said, still checking out the woman who was standing at the bottom of the steps.

As Freddie started down the steps, Emmy Lou smiled at him. Then, she reached into her jacket pocket and pulled out a gun. Without hesitation, she shot Freddie, who was still looking at her, right between the eyes.

About the Author

I was born in Idaho in 1939. My father's job demanded that we frequently move and, by the age of ten, I had lived in Idaho, Montana, Colorado, Michigan, and Wisconsin.

I am the proud mother of three wonderful sons and two fantastic grandsons. I have no plans to acquire another husband, as they are just too much work.

For most of my life, I worked as an accountant. Two years before I retired, I did a complete switch in careers and managed two Curves fitness facilities in Illinois. I retired in 2002 and moved to Branson, MO. In 2012, I moved to Indiana to be closer to my family and have resided in Highland since then.

I enjoy a good laugh and figure it's my sense of humor that keeps me going when times are tough. Reading has always been one of my passions and I still read a couple of books a week.

In 2014, I wrote my first book, *Blueberries and Bears and My Brother's Shoes*, a book about growing up in the forties and fifties. After I self-published it and gave it to friends and family to read, they encouraged me to get serious about my writing.

I never thought that, at the age of 76, I would become an author. I set a goal for myself to write at least ten books before I die. I've made the ten-plus and I'm pretty sure I have a lot more novels kicking around in this head of mine.

I certainly am enjoying my retirement knowing, that when I get up each morning, I have something to look forward to. You can find out more about me and my books at www.susanlpare.com. Please visit me there, sign up to be on my readers' list, and feel free to send me your comments.

www.ingramcontent.com/pod-product-compliance
Lightning Source LLC
Chambersburg PA
CBHW050734230626
47052CB00002BA/184